Murdered, My Sweet

Murdered, My Sweet

Joan Lowery Nixon

DELACORTE PRESS

Published by
Delacorte Press
Bantam Doubleday Dell Publishing Group, Inc.
1540 Broadway
New York, New York 10036

Library of Congress Cataloging-in-Publication Data
Nixon, Joan Lowery.
    Murdered, my sweet / Joan Lowery Nixon.
       p.   cm.
    Summary: Jenny and her mother hunt a killer while
fearing for their own safety, after the reading of their
millionaire cousin's will leads to the murder of another
cousin.
    ISBN 0-385-32245-3 (alk. paper)
    [1. Murder—Fiction.   2. Mystery and detective stories.]
I. Title.
PZ7.N65Mo   1997
[Fic]—dc20
                           96-43431
                           CIP
                           AC

The text of this book is set in 12-point Goudy.
Book design by Julie E. Baker

Manufactured in the United States of America
September 1997
10 9 8 7 6 5 4 3 2 1
BVG

Another one to Nick

Chapter One

It's not easy being related to a woman who's famous for murdering people.

Don't get me wrong. Mom's not a *real* murderer. She's Madeline Jakes, the most famous mystery writer in the United States—maybe the world. She's a good writer, too. I've never met anyone who could read one of Mom's novels late at night and not have to sleep with the bathroom light on.

So many people have seen Mom's picture on the back of her book jackets and watched her being interviewed on TV that they recognize her in public places. "There's Madeline Jakes!" some whisper. Some point. Maybe because they've been watching too much television, I notice some glance around to see if Mom's with the police, helping to solve a murder at that very moment.

Solve a murder? Mom? It's actually funny. My mom is a woman who half the time can't even figure out where she put her car keys or placed

1

her glasses. She rarely remembers birthdays or doctor appointments or speaking engagements unless she's reminded. Mom has never solved a murder in her life, except for the murders in her books. Because she makes those up, she knows from the very beginning "whodunnit." I don't count them.

Try telling that to Mom. She's actually started to believe what she reads about herself, because when fans ask her about real cases she's solved, she doesn't come right out and say, "What cases? The police have never once asked for my help." Instead she smiles as though she has a big secret. She even giggles, which is really gross behavior for a forty-three-year-old woman. When I hear her murmur something about classified information, I want to . . . well, just imagine!

"If I only had the chance, Jenny," Mom said to me recently, "I *know* I could use my skills as a mystery writer to solve real crimes."

"Mom," I reminded her, "it's your brother who solves real crimes. Uncle Bill's a homicide detective. You're a writer. You use your imagination and your computer to give your fans stories about make-believe murders."

Mom tapped a pencil against her nose, smiled, and gazed far away. "But if I had the chance to solve a real crime," she insisted, "I know I could."

It wouldn't have done any good to answer. I fought back the resentment that sometimes boils up and threatens to choke me when Mom goes off into her fictional world like one of her own characters. That's when, more than ever, I wish that Dad were still alive, because whenever Mom became a sailboat, Dad was there as an anchor. And sometimes I want to scream at Mom, "*You're* the mother, not *me*! You're supposed to be taking care of *me*! Why do I end up having to take care of *you*?"

Dad had been an officer in the Air Force, and we were transferred so much we were never able to make friends who were keepers. When I was little it didn't matter to me, because there were always kids around to play with, but Mom likes people and badly wanted friends, so everywhere we went she joined clubs and took classes in whatever was handy. That's how she became interested in writing. She signed up for a class in "How to Write a Mystery Novel," and found—as she told us—where she truly belonged.

Her books were published, but Mom didn't make much money with them for the first few years. And when Dad's plane crashed, Mom was so heartbroken I thought she'd never be able to write again. But Mom has always had courage and spunk, and one day she told me, "Jenny, if I work hard and write books that people want to read, I know that someday I can make a good life for you."

Maybe Mom knew all along that her books would be best-sellers and she'd be famous. And maybe somewhere inside her all along was the persona that blossomed overnight. A publicist advised her, "Don't go to interviews or talk shows as a pleasant neighbor-next-door. Your

3

public wants to see a writer of mysteries. That means glamour . . . drama . . . pizzazz!"

The chiffon scarves, the drama, and the "darlings" fit Mom like a beautiful new dress. I didn't mind at first. Mom had always been filled with imagination and fun. However, her new personality has a downside. It may be that the glamorous mystery writer is no longer able to handle all the mundane, routine details of life by herself. Or maybe she enjoys leaving them behind and joining the social life of many of the famous people she meets. Whatever the reason, I end up having to do a lot of the mothering. I'm too young to be a mother—especially my mother's mother—but there's nothing I can do about it.

In spite of having to deal with a mother who spends much of her life in never-never land, I love my mom. I really do, even during the moments when we seem to be trying to drive each other crazy.

When Mom's not mentally off somewhere inside the story she's writing, she's fun to be with, and often, when she goes away on weekends or holidays, for autographings or to give lectures, she takes me with her. I swim in the hotel pool or lie on the beach, and eat great food. When people smile and ask me, "Do you ever help your mother solve mysteries?" I answer, "I'm the one who helps her remember where she's going so she can catch her plane on time."

They think that's a great joke. Unfortunately for me it isn't a joke.

I've always liked to read mysteries. I think it's

4

because I love the challenge of spotting clues and figuring things out. I started reading Nancy Drews when I was seven. I soon graduated into young adult mysteries—stacks and stacks of them—and now I'm into some of Dad's old Raymond Chandler and John D. MacDonald stories, and Mom's Sue Grafton and Mary Higgins Clark novels.

I'm pretty good at figuring out whodunnit before the last big scene, but Mom never can. At first I thought that her mind went off in directions she'd take if *she* were writing the story. Or that she got sidetracked by the characters. Or that maybe she became too tangled in motives and means to recognize the crucial clue when she saw it. But I realized what the problem was when, one day, Mom showed me how she developed and put together the parts of a story.

Mom rarely asks me to help her talk out tough spots in her own books. When she's organizing and writing her stories, she's good. She follows the advice of the well-known *Perry Mason* mystery novelist, Erle Stanley Gardner. In plotting, Gardner wrote, approach the story from the viewpoint of the murderer. The advice works well for Mom when she plots her mystery stories. But it doesn't help her figure out the solution to other authors' mystery novels or to crimes that happen in real life because in those cases, you don't start with the murderer. You have to figure out who that person is.

Last week, right before my high school's April spring break, Mom finished writing *A Crack in the Computer,* her latest mystery novel starring amateur sleuth Audrey Downing. That meant she'd wait a few weeks before beginning the next novel, so when she asked, "Would you like to go to San Antonio?" right away I said, "Sure!" I love San Antonio's Riverwalk and Jim Cullum's terrific jazz band that plays most nights there, and the really fab food.

I made a mistake. If I'd known the reason for the trip, I probably would have tried to argue Mom out of going. If that hadn't worked, I would have begged to stay behind with my best friend, Traci, because the whole idea of our being in San Antonio was actually morbid.

It all had to do with Mom's cousin Arnold Harmony.

"First cousin, once removed," Mom always said. That meant he was really her father's much older first cousin, and Mom was the next generation along. I guess she had to keep saying that because Arnold Harmony was really ancient, and she wouldn't want people thinking she was anywhere near his age.

Harmony Chocolates is known across the United States because most folks have probably pigged out on Harmony Chocolates at least once in their lives. They have an awful singing commercial—"Harmony Chocolates—a song in every bite"—that gets into your mind at the worst possible times and won't leave until you start humming "Ninety-nine bottles of beer on the wall," or "Look for the Union Label," or any jingle just as hard to shake, once you've heard it.

Arnold Harmony, who founded the company, should have just continued making and selling chocolates. But at the age of almost eighty-eight, Arnold decided to rewrite his will and have the new will read to his guests at a slam-bang birthday party.

Mom insisted that the least we could do, after enjoying the box of Harmony Chocolates we were sent at Christmas each year, was to accept Arnold's invitation and attend his party.

"Is he going to leave you some money? Is that why he wants you to be there when the will is read?" I asked Mom.

"Oh, gracious no. There's Claudine—his wife—a son named Porter, and a grandson named Logan. I'm sure they'll inherit his company and his money." Mom smiled tenderly. "Dear, dear Arnold. Years ago, when I was a little girl, he told me that someday he'd give me Agnes's musical teapot. I've always had happy memories of visits I made to Arnold and Agnes's with my mother when I was a little girl. Agnes served us tea from that dear little teapot with its pink roses and tiny violets. I'm sure that's why he invited me to hear the will."

A billionaire promises my mom a *teapot,* and it makes her happy? I guess that's one of the things I really truly love about her. Of course, she makes money from her mystery novels, but not even close to the riches of Harmony Chocolates.

"Who's Agnes, Mom?" I asked. "I thought you said Arnold's wife is Claudine."

"His present wife," Mom explained. "Agnes

7

died a little over ten years ago. I didn't get her teapot then, but maybe it was because we had to miss the funeral. I'm afraid that the Harmonys and the Jakeses just haven't kept up with each other the way we should."

"Well, you're going to your cousin's birthday party," I said, "and that should please him."

When we arrived on Saturday in San Antonio, we checked into a large, comfortable hotel on the Paseo del Rio—the Riverwalk—and unpacked, putting all our things in the drawers and tucking our suitcases out of sight in the closet. Mom's a neat freak, which probably comes from years of lining up clues and red herrings and keeping them straight. It's easier for me to go along with it than make a mess and have to deal with a semihysterical mother.

Our room overlooked a busy, colorful slice of the Riverwalk, which was fine with me. I opened the sliding glass doors and stepped onto a narrow little balcony. Leaning on the low railing, I could look down eight stories, past rows of small balconies, and watch the people below me. April in San Antonio means festival and flowers. The city couldn't have been prettier.

I was able to sneak in a swim and a shower before Mom announced it was time to dress for Cousin Arnold's reception, which was to be held in the Magnolia Suite on the second floor of this hotel.

"Why not at his house?" I asked. "He lives in a mansion in San Antonio, doesn't he?"

"It's a comfortable home, but not a mansion,"

Mom corrected me. "Arnold never was one for pretensions. I doubt that it has enough bedrooms for his out-of-town guests."

As we got off the hotel elevator on the floor where the reception was to be held, I gave a last, wishful glance out the large window to the Riverwalk, with its swarm of brightly costumed people in sequined shawls, ribbon-trimmed full skirts, and decorated sombreros—out to celebrate San Antonio's annual Battle of the Flowers parade.

Traci would love this, I thought. *I'll send her a postcard.* Then I dutifully trailed along in Mom's wake until we reached the Magnolia Suite.

A well-dressed man stood outside the door, scowling to himself. He was probably in his late fifties. He had thin, graying hair and eyebrows that looked like they were doing the Wave. His main interest seemed to be pacing in the hallway, so he hadn't noticed Mom and me.

"Porter? Is that you?" Mom asked, and the man started.

Mom beamed as she put an arm around my shoulders, lightly shoving me forward. "Porter, darling, this is my daughter, Jennifer," she said.

I murmured something polite, but he kept his scowl and nodded, then peered through his heavy-rimmed glasses. He attempted a weak smile. "Madeline," Porter said in a quiet tone, "I'm glad you're here. You're just the person I need to talk to."

"About what, dear?" Mom asked.

I noticed Porter glance over his shoulder

9

toward the door to the Magnolia Suite. Maybe it was my imagination, but I thought I saw him shudder.

"Later," he said. "After this farce is over tonight, we can talk with more privacy."

"Let's go in and join the party," Mom said, but Porter shook his head.

"There've been too many parties," he mumbled. "Something must be done."

Chapter Two

The door suddenly opened, and a blond woman, glittering from lots of really big diamonds, stood in the entrance. She looked at Mom without smiling and completely ignored Porter. "You're Madeline Jakes," she said. "I'm Claudine Harmony. Arnold will be delighted to see you."

Mom gently pushed me forward. "And this is my daughter, Jennifer."

Claudine acknowledged me with a slight nod and held open the door to the suite, waiting for us to enter. We followed her into an immense, elegant room with polished tables, muted gold wallpaper, and a huge, glittery chandelier. Claudine looked about Mom's age. Mom is really attractive with her dark hair and deep blue eyes, which fortunately came along to me in the genes department. She looked great in a blue-and-green chiffon dress with a matching scarf that she liked to wear when she was being interviewed. I didn't look so bad myself. Mom lets me buy the kind of clothes I like when I need them.

Claudine ushered us to a huge dark-brown leather wing chair. I realized it was Cousin Arnold I saw wrapped in a deep red robe, with a brown blanket over his legs. He looked like a wrinkled cherry tucked inside its chocolate covering.

Claudine said, "Here is Madeline, my love, with her daughter, Jessie."

"Jenny," I corrected. "Happy birthday."

A tough and twisted birdlike claw emerged from the blanket and grasped my hand. "Jenny," he said. "How old are you, Jenny? Nineteen? Twenty?"

"Fifteen," I answered, immensely flattered.

"Well, be a good girl and mind your mother," he said. Then he turned his attention to Mom and seemed to forget I was there. I plopped down in a chair near one of the windows and glanced around the room.

Other guests had arrived. Nearby I saw a blond, lightly tanned man who was dressed in stonewashed jeans, a white dress shirt, and a navy blazer. I knew he was definitely twenty or over. What I didn't know was why he was glaring at me.

"Hi," I said, trying to be friendly. He just nodded, turning his gaze to the activity outside the window.

I walked over to join him. "I'm Jennifer Jakes," I said. "Hi."

"I know who you are." He almost grunted the words out.

I wasn't about to let him get away with that. I asked, "I didn't catch your name?"

"Logan," he mumbled. "Logan Harmony."

"You're Cousin Arnold's grandson. Right?"

There was no one else to talk to, so I tried another topic. "Look at the tourist boats floating down the river in the sunlight," I said. "The people on the boats look so relaxed and happy. I've never ridden on the boats, but I'd like to. Maybe after this reading of the will—"

"Listen, I don't mean to be rude but my grandfather should have had more sense," Logan mumbled in such a low tone of voice I wasn't sure I'd heard him correctly. "Reading his will to guests is stupid. It's crass. Besides that, it's dangerous."

"Dangerous?" I asked.

Someone laughed at something Arnold had said, and Logan twisted to glance.

"Of course it's dangerous," he answered. "At this reception my grandfather plans to tell us how he's going to *change* his will. Then tonight, after dinner, he'll sign the damned thing in front of everyone. Crass. Crazy. No one's pleased with this. Some of the people involved are downright angry. One in particular . . ."

He broke off as though he suddenly realized he should be quiet. He looked toward my mom and back to me again.

I knew he was thinking about Mom being on close terms with the police. "Don't worry," I said. "My mom is only interested in one thing—a teapot."

Logan started and his eyes flew wide open. "*Teapot?* What are you talking about?" he asked. His expression was a mixture of suspicion and confusion.

I realized that I shouldn't have brought up even a part of what Mom had told me about her girlhood and the musical teapot. It must have sounded dumb. "I'm sorry. I shouldn't have said anything," I said.

I walked away from the window and sat down, waiting for Mom.

From the corner of my eye I saw Logan beckon to a woman who was wearing too much makeup. She didn't look like a twenty-year-old, but a silly forty-year-old with an overdone face. Her red hair and its style were right out of a fashion magazine. I wouldn't have even tried to guess how much her designer dress cost. It was obvious, from the great shape she was in, that she worked out on a regular basis. She might even be one of those people who has a personal trainer.

Logan said something to her that I couldn't hear. I watched her red-red lips open, and out exploded the words, "*Teapot?* How could she possibly know?"

Apparently I'd said the wrong thing. What was such a big deal about a little musical teapot?

The woman strolled purposefully in my direction, so I stood up and smiled.

To my surprise, she smiled back. "Hi," she said. "I'm Alexa Blair, Arnold Harmony's—"

"Secretary," Logan said.

Alexa didn't even blink. "Personal business

14

manager," she said. "I began four years ago as a secretary, but now I handle Mr. Harmony's personal business affairs."

"You must be the person who sends Mom and me a box of Harmony Chocolates every Christmas," I said.

She laughed, as though she and I shared a joke. "That's just a small part of my job," she said. "Mr. Harmony is generous with charitable contributions. I represent his interests at many fund-raisers, both local and national."

"That's great," I said. I like thinking of Cousin Arnold as a generous man. Mom's generous, too. Maybe generosity runs in the family, and I've also got those genes, although I haven't had enough of my own money to find out yet.

"I'm looking forward to meeting your mother," Alexa told me. "I love her books. I'm such a devoted fan that I snatch them up as soon as they're published. She must get tired of hearing people tell her what a terrific writer she is."

"Not so you'd notice," I replied. "Feel free to tell her."

"I understand she's helped the police solve quite a few mysteries."

Alexa was obviously waiting for me to answer. I just smiled. I remembered how those foolish rumors first got started, but I don't think anyone else makes the connection. About the time that Mom's mystery novels started climbing onto best-seller lists, TV viewers were glued to a television show about a woman mystery novelist who solves mysteries with the police—sometimes in

15

spite of the police. Mom, who had become a dramatic mystery writer like the TV character was, got connected in people's minds with solving cases. It's as if it were part of Mom's job description.

Magazine articles and television interviews that promote Mom's books often include questions about whether or not she helps the police. Mom never says *no*. Instead she gets coy, raises one eyebrow, and acts like she really does help the police, but it's a big secret. Now people think she's just like that fictional mystery writer who was on TV.

Sometimes it really gets to me, but I never tell Mom.

"Do you live here in San Antonio?" I asked Alexa, changing the subject.

"I have a little condominium in the hills," she replied quickly. "But let's not bother with chitchat. I'd rather get down to business. I've heard that you've mentioned the teapot."

"I shouldn't have said anything about the teapot," I answered. "You'll have to talk to my mom."

Alexa looked at me long and hard. "Your mother really is a good detective. I didn't know how good."

"I can't figure out how she got hold of the code word," Logan mumbled to himself as much as to Alexa.

"What?" I asked.

I could see Alexa's fingers press on Logan's arm, trying to get him to be quiet, but he leaned toward me and burst out, "Don't bother looking innocent and pretending you don't know what we're talking about. You can tell your mother to forget it. The deal's off. It wouldn't fly. It fell through."

This was the strangest conversation I'd ever had. I decided the best thing was to go along with whatever he had in mind. "So it's over," I said.

"That's it," Logan said.

"We won't talk about it again," I told him, hoping I was right.

"We won't. But you tell your mother about our conversation," Alexa said. "Fill her in. Make sure she understands."

"Will she understand?"

"There's no point in your mother discussing this with her police associates or anyone else. As you said, it's over, and it's none of their business, either."

"Okay," I said, wondering what in the world we were talking about. Alexa didn't know that Mom doesn't have any police associates in San Antonio. Even in Houston, where we live, there's just Uncle Bill, who answers all Mom's questions about police procedure and makes sure everything she writes about it is accurate. Alexa didn't even know about Uncle Bill, because he'd never been close to the Harmonys.

I felt so uncomfortable, I tried to say something to Logan to lighten the situation. "We met your father," I told him.

"I don't call him *father*. Porter and I do not

have a father-son relationship," Logan snapped. What I had said suddenly hit him, and he asked, "Are you telling us that Porter's the one who brought your mother here, and not grandfather?"

"I'm not telling you anything," I said. I was totally bewildered and felt like I had walked in on the middle of a movie, not knowing what was going on.

Alexa squeezed Logan's arm even more tightly. "Jenny is simply reminding you that we agreed not to talk about it. Now run along. Relax. Get something to eat and drink."

As Logan strode off, a little wobbly on his feet, a spindly little woman with tight white curls stepped up and wrapped her fingers around Alexa's arm. Squinting into her face, she said, "Janie, dear, you're the spitting image of your mother."

"I'm Janie," I told her. "I mean, I'm Jenny. I think you mean me. My mother is Madeline Jakes."

She turned and stared, her face just a few inches from mine. "Well, so you are," she said. "Unfortunately, I don't have my glasses on. I'm a cousin on Arnold's other side of the family—Elsie Dean."

She pulled me aside until we reached a couple of chairs where we could sit down. Apparently Alexa had nothing more to say to me. She walked through the growing crowd to the other side of the room.

"Are all the people here related to Arnold Harmony?" I asked.

"Oh, no," she answered. "Some are distant cousins, like you and me, but most are employees of Harmony Chocolates."

"That's interesting," I said politely.

"The idea of this party is stupid. The whole thing is going to be boring," she said, almost giggling. "I take the *boring* part back. It might be fun to see the faces of the people mentioned in the will, depending on what Arnold leaves them. He's made some *changes*, you know."

"That's what my mom told me."

Elsie Dean leaned toward me, her voice almost a whisper. "Some of them may be happy with the changes, but for others—mark my words—it's going to be murder!"

Chapter Three

❥

Elsie asked me to get her a cup of punch, so I did. When I returned, a well-padded woman was seated in my chair. Elsie introduced her as Mabel Hopper, her younger sister. Mabel wore a small, shiny straw hat. It poked out at all angles, and was the same exact shade as her dyed black hair, so she gave the impression of having a really weird hairdo. Mabel kept happily bobbing her head as she smiled at me, and her chins rippled up and down.

"Is your lovely famous mother here for business or pleasure?" Mabel asked me.

That was a strange question, and I didn't know how to answer it, so I said, "She's here because Cousin Arnold invited her."

Mabel nodded again, this time at Elsie. "He hired her for protection," she said. "I knew it."

"Protection against what?" I asked.

"Against what might happen when Arnold's will is read," Mabel answered.

Elsie gave a kind of harrumph. "Arnold still

20

has a sharp mind. I think he wants to show some of the family members who take him and his money for granted that he's well aware of who they are and what they've been doing."

I couldn't help asking. "Who are these family members and what have they been doing?"

"Goodness, how should we know?" Elsie answered. "We haven't even seen Arnold since Christmas Day five years ago."

Mabel nodded again. "And we don't gossip." She patted her ample stomach. "But speaking of Arnold's hospitality, that was the worst Christmas dinner I've ever eaten. Claudine carries this healthy eating business much too far. No gravy, no stuffing, no—"

I murmured my excuses and walked away from them. It helped to remind myself that Elsie had said that she and Mabel were on Arnold's other side of the family.

Just then, Mom glanced around, spotted me, and held out a hand. As I joined her, a tall man, perfectly dressed in a well-cut dark blue business suit, stepped onto a low platform near the fireplace and began to fiddle with a microphone.

"Now that all the guests have arrived . . . ," he began. The mike squealed, and everyone winced, so he tried adjusting it.

"Who's he?" I asked Mom.

"His name is Booth Dockman," Mom answered. "He's Arnold's attorney. According to what Arnold told me a few minutes ago, Harmony Chocolates is Booth's biggest client."

Mr. Dockman tried the mike again, and this

time his voice came across strong and clear. He attempted a smile. It was obvious he didn't like what he had to do.

"Ladies and gentlemen," he said again, "may I please have your attention?"

He hadn't needed to ask. Everyone in the room had been patiently waiting for him.

"Thank you," Mr. Dockman said. "As all of you know, I represent Mr. Arnold Harmony, president and chairman of the board of Harmony Chocolates."

Mr. Dockman cleared his throat a couple of times before he was able to continue. Finally, he said, "You are aware that Mr. Harmony has arranged a dinner party to follow this reception. After the dinner party Mr. Harmony's will, updated with revisions and extensions, and—"

"Get on with it, Booth," Arnold called out.

At this Mr. Dockman's face kind of twisted. He looked very unhappy about having to do this.

"It may seem a bit unusual to some of you, but Mr. Harmony expressed his desire to have the will read while he was still in energetic good health and could enjoy the event, not at some time in the far distant future after he has departed this life," Mr. Dockman said. He choked into a coughing fit, then managed to blurt out, "Please have a good time at the reception. Dinner will be served in the Fiesta Room promptly at seven-thirty. We'll see you all there."

There was silence for a moment. Then Logan Harmony called out, "Why wait until after dinner, Grandfather? Why not read the will now?"

Arnold chuckled and answered, "The will has to be read after dinner because it's the dessert. You might call it the *just* desserts."

I heard Mabel say, "Oh, darn. I was hoping we'd get those chocolate mousse thingies this hotel is famous for."

Elsie shushed her, and most of the people in the room seemed to pretend they hadn't heard, but I couldn't help it. Before I knew what I was doing, I laughed. Mr. Dockman looked shocked, and Logan turned and gave me a dirty look, but Arnold laughed, too, and winked at me.

He tottered to his feet, and a stocky, white-coated attendant suddenly appeared with a wheelchair. "Thank you, Adam," Arnold said. He gave a wave to his guests. "Enjoy the rest of the reception and the dinner party. I'll see you here after dinner."

Adam wheeled him away.

There were about twenty people in the room. They stood in self-conscious clusters, not speaking, not even knowing where to look. I leaned into Mom and whispered, "We've got to talk."

"Of course, dear," Mom said. "But I won't be able to hear you unless you speak up."

"I can't. We have to talk privately."

Mom flung her scarf back across one shoulder and rose gracefully, meanwhile sweeping the room with her glance and her smile. She strode down the hall and into the elevator, the scarf and skirt of her dress swirling after her. I trotted a couple of paces behind.

"That's Madeline Jakes!" some people whispered.

Mom pretended that she hadn't heard, but smiled like a queen to everyone in the elevator.

Once we were finally inside our room, she kicked off her shoes and flopped into a nearby armchair. "All right, Jennifer, my sweet," she said to me. "What's all this mysterious 'We've got to talk' business?"

"Alexa Blair and Logan Harmony asked me to talk to you. Did you meet them?"

"I didn't have a chance to speak to either of them, but I'd met Logan, when he was much, much younger—about eight or ten. He still has that pouty, scowly, little spoiled-boy look. I'd recognize him anywhere."

Her eyes lit up and she said, "Like one of the minor characters I'm going to use in my next book." She pulled a small notebook and pen from her handbag and began to write. "Pouty, scowly," she said. "Oh, that's good. I like that. I—"

"Mom," I said. "Right now forget your book. We have to talk about Logan and Alexa. Do you know who Alexa is?"

Mom smiled as she put away her notebook and pen. "Oh, yes," she said. "I've written about her type of character dozens of times. Beautiful in a flashy way, decorates the office where she works, usually knows something she eventually spills to Audrey Downing, who's working to solve the crime."

"Get real for a minute, Mom," I said, and

struggled to keep from losing my patience. "Audrey Downing is fictional. She's your series character. What I'm going to tell you is not in one of your books. Alexa and Logan said some very strange things to me, and they asked me to repeat them to you."

Mom sat upright, blinked a couple of times as if coming in for an earth landing, and said, "I'm sorry, sweetie. Please tell me what's bothering you. I'm listening."

I went over the details about the teapot, as well as I could remember them, and after I finished, I waited while Mom thought about it.

Finally, she said, "They called *teapot* a code word, so there's the possibility it has something to do with computers. In my novel *A Crack in the Computer*, Audrey—"

I couldn't take getting sidetracked again. I wanted to jump up and down and yell that we weren't in one of Mom's stories, but I hung on to my temper and said, "It could have to do with computers, or it could refer to some corporate business thing."

"Corporate problems. Good idea. We'll find out," Mom said, and smiled at me, preening a little at the same time. "Isn't it interesting that Logan and Alexa remarked that I was a very good detective and wondered how I got hold of the code word."

"They think you're working with either Arnold or Porter, and they don't want you to go with this to the police," I said.

"Hmmm." Mom rubbed her chin as she

thought. "Why would I go to the police about a teapot? First I'd have to break the code and find out what *Teapot* means."

"Right now it doesn't mean anything. They said it was over, that the deal was off."

"That could mean it failed," Mom countered. "Or it could be a lie intended to divert our suspicions."

"It wouldn't fly," I quoted. "The deal fell through."

"It's over," Mom murmured, remembering. Then she said, "For the two of them, maybe, but not for us. They've whetted my curiosity, and I'll go to the police with this if I darned well want to."

I flung myself across the bed. "Go to the police with what?" I shouted. "We don't know what they were talking about! I don't even know what you and I are talking about! Do you?"

"Sweetie, you're going to wrinkle your dress," Mom said. "Falling apart in the face of a challenge won't do. Sit up and behave yourself."

I groaned, but I did what she said.

Mom had risen to her feet. "Our next step," she told me, "is to have a nice chat with Alexa. . . . Yes, Alexa. Her type eventually tells all. If I had a bit more information . . ."

She got up and checked her lipstick in the mirror. "I also have to talk with Porter. I wonder what he wants to see me about. Something is obviously worrying him." She smiled and added, "I doubt if he's mixed up in teapots, too."

I shrugged. By this time I didn't care about

teapots. Mom might find out something interesting enough to use in her next mystery novel, but I was out of it. The teapot deal wouldn't fly? Well, neither would I.

"We've got only about half an hour left of the reception," Mom said. "We'd better hurry back."

"You go ahead," I said. "I've got to brush my hair. I'll be down in a minute."

"All right," Mom said. "Just remember to be prompt for dinner. Seven-thirty, no later. And no excuses."

"Mom," I said, "believe me. I'll be on time."

Chapter Four

I leisurely put myself together. Then I ambled down the hall to the elevator block, stopping to look again at the Fiesta scene below. Multiple strings of colored lights glittered in the dusk, and the crowds who had left the parade route were pouring out like bright streamers along the Riverwalk. A decorated flatboat leisurely slid by, and I could see that the people on it were seated around a table, scarfing down Casa Rio enchiladas.

Envious, I said aloud to myself, "I'd so much rather be on one of those boats, eating really good food, than having to go to Arnold Harmony's dinner."

"It wouldn't be much fun if you had to work on the boats," a voice said. "Especially in July and August when the sun is killer hot."

I turned around and saw a guy dressed as a bellman, with an empty luggage cart behind him. He grinned at me and said, "Last summer, when I was sixteen, my uncle got me a job working the boats as a waiter."

As good looks go, this guy was the max. Traci would have agreed to that. Tall, with big brown eyes and curly dark hair; there wasn't one thing I'd check for "needs improvement."

I knew I was gaping, so I smiled and said something that was supposed to be brilliant but came out stupid. "So now you work at the hotel."

"Weekends and holidays only," he said. "I'm still in school." He paused, then said, "Your name is Jennifer Jakes. One of the front-desk clerks pointed out your mother when you checked into the hotel. The clerk was so excited she kept saying she thought she might faint."

"Did she?"

"I don't know," he said. "I was looking at you."

I felt myself blushing, which is probably the most uncool thing I can think of, but I felt better when I saw that his face turned kind of red, too.

"We get a lot of celebrities here, major and minor," he said. "Tonight we've got a movie producer scouting out a location, and a college basketball team."

"Word must get around the hotel fast."

"I make it a point to know who checks in," he said. "There's a columnist at the *San Antonio Light* who tips for information he can use." He grinned. "Your mom should be worth a couple of bucks."

Just then the elevator *down* light flashed, and a soft *ding* sounded.

As the doors opened I stepped in, pressing to one side to make room for the cart. Thankfully we were the only ones in the elevator.

"While you're here this weekend, Jennifer, if you need anything, ask for me—Carlos. Carlos Martinez. If you just say 'Carlos,' they'll know who you mean."

"Okay," I said. "And call me Jenny." We reached the second floor, where the reception areas were. Just before the doors slid wide, Carlos gave me a great big smile that kept my spirits up all the way to Arnold's reception.

I walked into the Magnolia Suite, just ahead of a waiter in formal attire who tapped out some notes on soft chimes and announced that dinner was ready to be served in the Fiesta Room.

Mom had been talking to Logan. As they walked toward the door, following the waiter, I heard her say, "Perhaps it's just a matter of finding yourself, darling. I've heard that sometimes a string of failures leads to eventual success. However, that unfortunate motorcycle incident in Las Vegas . . ."

Motorcycle incident? The way Logan was glaring at Mom, I was pretty sure that if she wanted any information about *Teapot* from him, she wasn't going to get it.

I fell into step with Mom, and Logan edged back, disappearing inside the crush of hungry bodies as we moved through the hallway to the Fiesta Room.

The round tables that filled the room were beautifully decorated with stunning flowers, silver candelabra, and tall, thin, white candles. There was arranged seating, so I found my place card and ended up sitting between Elsie Dean and a large, stocky man whose name was Gustave Gunter. I began to think of him as Gustave *Grunter*, because each time he spoke, a bushy gray mustache rose like a curtain and his heavily accented words spilled out in sharp staccato bursts. Elsie and Gustave spoke over my head, as though I didn't count since I was only a teenager. I listened and learned that Gustave was not a Harmony relative, but a vice president of Harmony Chocolates.

It was not a good week for Gustave. A bunion on his foot hurt, he was facing a root canal, and he was very upset with Arnold for revising the will.

"Someone's behind it," Gustave grumbled as the waiter removed what was left of our salads. "I don't like this sudden change on Arnold's part or his strange attitude. Believe me, someone's influenced him."

"No one's ever been able to influence Arnold," Elsie said. "He's only influenced by facts and figures." She bent over and peered at the entrée that had been put down in front of her. "Chicken," she said in disgust. "Have you ever been to a hotel dinner that didn't include chicken?" Apparently forgiving the hotel, she picked up her knife and fork and attacked the chicken. Melted butter spurted out, spotting her dress and the tablecloth, but she didn't seem to notice.

Alexa squeezed past our table, bumping my chair. I looked up and glanced around, surprised. "Not everybody's here," I said.

Elsie stared at me, surprised. "Alexa was probably going to the ladies' room."

"I mean there are empty places at most of the tables. Like ours. Who's supposed to be sitting across from me?"

Elsie picked up the place card, held it close to her nose, and read, "Porter Harmony."

"See what I mean?" I asked. "His salad's still sitting there, and he hasn't shown up." I stretched to look around as Logan slipped into the room and into a chair at a table across from my mother.

Gustave and Elsie went back to discussing ill health, ignoring what I had pointed out, but I kept watch. Claudine left the room, then returned, talking to Alexa. Claudine left again, as Booth Dockman returned. Alexa went out, but I soon saw her going from table to table, socializing with the other guests. Gustave wolfed down his meal, threw down his napkin, then left the table without excusing himself.

"He's really in a bad mood," I said to Elsie.

She nodded and said, "Painful bunions affect the entire nervous system."

I poked around on my plate, not terribly hungry and not looking forward to what was going to follow. Reading wills was not only boring, but it was getting more and more depressing. If it weren't for Mom, I'd have skipped the whole thing and telephoned Traci or found out if Carlos had a few minutes off duty.

Finally Booth—I was sure I'd seen him leave—startled me by standing up at the far end of the room, next to Gustave. He announced that we were all invited to return to the Magnolia Suite for the reading of the will.

"Hummph! No chocolate mousse!" I heard Mabel complain. This time it didn't strike me as funny. This whole situation was beyond funny.

It took only ten or fifteen minutes for us to assemble back in the Magnolia Suite, where many of us took chairs that had been set in three rows facing an ornate desk. As if we were obeying an unspoken rule, none of us claimed chairs in the first row, saving them for the immediate family. I grabbed Mom's arm and pulled her into the third row. I wanted to be near a friendly face.

With a squeal of happiness, Mabel discovered a side table with coffee, tea, and "the little chocolate mousse thingies" she'd been pining for. Elsie joined her.

Claudine sauntered in, stopped to speak to a few of the guests, and sat alone in the front row. Logan plopped into the chair at the right end of that row, keeping an empty chair between Claudine and himself. Logan sat slumped over, his long legs out in the aisle. I couldn't tell if he looked mad or sad, but it wasn't a pretty sight.

Alexa slipped into the seat just behind Logan, but Gustave surprised me by claiming the front row seat on the left side. Before he sat down, he stood as stiff as an army officer. His gaze swept the room, daring anyone to eject him from one of the supposed seats of honor.

Booth Dockman sat behind the large desk, a closed briefcase before him. He looked at his watch, drummed his fingers on the desk, then looked at his watch again.

"When do we get started?" Elsie asked loudly.

Booth didn't answer her question. He looked around the room and said, "Ladies and gentlemen, I apologize for the delay. Naturally, since Mr. Arnold Harmony planned this entire event around the public reading of his will, I don't want to begin until he gets here. It's very important to him to be present, and—"

Alexa broke in. "I think the whole idea is morbid," she said.

Claudine whirled to face Alexa. "It doesn't matter at all what *you* think, Miss Blair. It's Arnold's will. He can make any arrangement he wishes."

"I know that," Alexa said. "I just can't help wondering how in the world he's going to enjoy sitting there listening to Booth read off the legal terms. What are we supposed to do? Look sad? Like he was already dead?" She shuddered and made a face of disgust.

Booth scowled at her. "Alexa . . . Miss Blair, you are completely out of order."

Gustave interrupted. "Out of order, maybe, but correct," he said. "I agree with Miss Blair."

"Neither of you has any right to express an opinion." Claudine's hands fluttered nervously.

I jumped as Adam, Arnold Harmony's attendant, thundered past us and up to Booth's desk. "Mr. Dockman!" he bellowed.

Booth seemed startled, too, but he recovered and said to all of us, "Apparently Mr. Harmony is ready to join us."

"No, he's not," Adam said.

Looking almost as flustered as Claudine, Booth asked, "Did he say when to expect him?"

"Listen to me. Listen to me, please," Adam said. "I'm trying to tell you . . . there's been a murder."

A couple of people shrieked. Logan tottered to his feet and gasped, "Grandfather? Murdered?"

Claudine managed to stand, but all color drained from her face. "Arnold!" she murmured. "Oh, poor Arnold!"

As she crumpled to the floor, Adam stared at us with a bewildered look on his face. "Not Arnold Harmony," he said. "It's Porter Harmony, his son."

"P-Porter's been m-murdered?" Booth stammered. "How do you know? Are you sure?"

"I'm sure. You can believe me," Adam said. His big barrel chest heaved and rolled as he gave a humongous sigh and added, "I'm the one who found the body."

Chapter Five

❧

With a cry Logan bolted out of the room. A few others wavered in place as though they were about to leave, so Mom took over. Murder was something she knew about. Not that she'd ever been involved in one, but she knew what her characters would do. "Everyone calm down," she ordered majestically. "Adam, are you a nurse?"

"Yes, ma'am," he answered.

"Then please see what you can do for Claudine. Booth, if you have a phone in that briefcase, please call 911. Jenny, use the house phone over there to call the hotel operator. Ask her to send a security guard to completely secure the scene of the crime." She paused and asked, "What room was Porter in, Adam?"

He looked up from where he was kneeling next to Claudine. "Suite 485," he said, "next to Mr. Arnold's suite, 487."

As Booth and I began our calls, I heard Mom

tell everyone, "Please be seated. The police will want to talk to all of you."

They listened and obeyed.

"The minute I set eyes on Madeline, I knew something was going to happen," Elsie said. "Remember that woman mystery writer on TV? Every last one of her relatives were always being arrested and sent to jail."

Mabel gasped. "We won't have to go to jail, will we, Elsie?"

"Of course you won't," Mom said, with a comforting smile. "I won't allow it."

Won't allow it? Uh-oh, I thought. I could tell from the expression on Mom's face that mystery novelist Madeline Jakes was slipping into her sleuthing character, Audrey Downing.

It seemed to take forever for the operator to answer the phone. Finally, she went through her memorized happy greetings and asked, "How may I help you?"

"There's been a murder in suite 485," I said. "Please send one of your security people there right away." I glanced over at Booth, who had finished his call and was folding up his cellular phone. He looked awful—sort of like Swiss cheese does when it's been forgotten for a while and starts to mildew.

"Who is this?" the operator asked me.

"Jenny Jakes," I said.

"Jeanie, honey, it's not nice to play practical jokes on the phone," she said. "Be a good girl and turn on the TV to amuse yourself."

I put on the most formal voice I could and said, "I'm calling at the request of my mother, Madeline Jakes. As I informed you, there has been a murder."

The operator gasped. "Madeline Jakes? The author?"

She murmured something to someone in the room with her. All I heard was, "Madeline Jakes . . . She said there was a murder. . . . You were right. . . . Wherever she goes . . ."

"Will you please send someone from security to suite 485?" I asked again.

"Yes, ma'am, immediately," she answered, so I thanked her and hung up the phone.

Adam stood up. "Mrs. Harmony's all right. She just fainted," he said. "Would someone here rub her hands and put wet cloths on her face? I should get back to Mr. Arnold."

"How is Arnold taking the news?" Mom asked.

"He doesn't know yet," Adam said. "He had a light supper, then his nap. He's still asleep."

"If he wakes, don't tell him," Mom said. "Claudine should be with him, and probably his doctor."

Adam nodded, and Mom said, "How did you happen to find the body, Adam?"

"I saw that the door to Mr. Porter's suite was ajar, so I opened it. Mr. Porter's body was right there in the living room. I could see it from the entry hall. I went inside so I could check to see if there were any vital signs, and there weren't. I hope what I did was all right."

"You did exactly the right thing," Mom said, "but you'd better get back to Arnold." As Adam left the room, Mom glanced down at Claudine. "I suppose we should try to rouse her."

"I'll take care of that," Alexa said. She smiled as she picked up a carafe of ice water and aimed its flow at Claudine's head.

Claudine gave a yelp and sat up, water dripping down her hair. "You didn't have to do that!" she snapped at Alexa.

Mom immediately stepped in. "Claudine, dear, we are all unnerved by what has happened. I'm sure that Alexa had nothing but good intentions."

Mabel leaned toward me and said in a stage whisper, "Good intentions, my foot!"

Elsie nodded. "Claudine and Alexa have never been on good terms. I suspect Claudine wonders if Alexa got her job as Arnold's personal business manager because of her brains or her good looks."

"Wonders? Don't be silly," Mabel said. "Claudine knows."

As she got to her feet, Claudine sneered at Alexa and said, "I'm going to join my husband. I'll be in our suite."

"No, you won't," Mom said firmly. "We're all going to remain here until the police arrive."

"But my hair!"

"There are towels in the little bathroom over there," Mom answered. "And inside your small handbag are a comb, a compact, and a lipstick.

You have all that you need for now to make yourself presentable. You do intend to cooperate with the police, don't you?"

Claudine clutched her handbag to her chest with both hands, as though suspecting Mom might snatch it away. "How do you know what I have in my handbag?" she challenged.

Mom just raised one eyebrow and smiled enigmatically. I love using the word *enigmatic*. The definition—perplexing, mysterious—fits Mom so perfectly. I memorized the word when I had to know it for a vocabulary drill last year.

"What did I tell you, Mabel?" Elsie's whisper could be heard all over the room. "Madeline's a good detective. She'll take care of us and solve the crime."

I wanted to groan aloud. What was the matter with these people? A lot of women carry a comb, a compact, and a lipstick in their handbag. It wasn't great detecting on Mom's part to figure that out.

Claudine didn't say another word. She just headed for the bathroom and shut the door hard.

"I'm worried about Logan," Mom said to no one in particular.

Elsie answered. "Logan and his stepfather weren't on very good terms, Madeline. As a matter of fact, it was always my opinion that they couldn't stand each other."

"Stepfather?" I asked. "I didn't know that Porter was Logan's stepfather. Where's Logan's mother?"

"Oh, let me tell," Mabel said to Elsie. "You

always get it mixed up." Mabel took a deep breath that caused her to puff up like a balloon and rapidly exhale her words. "Logan was not even a year old when his mother married Porter. Her name was Linda. . . . Linda Something-or-other."

"Her name was Lydia," Elsie snapped. "Lydia Jane Smith. Now who's getting things mixed up?"

"Shouldn't somebody get in touch with Lydia?" I asked.

"Porter has tried to for the last fifteen years," Mabel answered.

"She disappeared?"

"Unfortunately Lydia left Porter while on a trip to the Caribbean," Elsie said.

"For another man," Mabel said. "She left a note."

"No, she didn't," Elsie insisted. "She just disappeared. Remember? There was some talk about her vanishing in the mysterious Bermuda Triangle."

"She wasn't anywhere near Bermuda," Mabel said.

The main doors to the suite swung open, and a tall man strode through a group of onlookers who had gathered in the hallway. I spotted Carlos for just an instant, but as the tall man entered our suite, he shut the doors firmly behind him.

He had lots of gray-streaked brown hair, and his wrinkled business suit was tight across the shoulders and chest. In a rugged, older-man kind of way you could say he was good looking. Alexa and Mom looked at him the way Mabel had stared at the chocolate mousse, so I guess they thought so, too. He glanced around the room, and since Mom was the only one standing, he walked toward her, holding out a worn leather folder with his police badge and I.D.

"I'm Detective Sergeant Sam Donovan, with San Antonio's homicide division. I'm looking for a Madeline Jakes."

"I'm Madeline Jakes," Mom trilled and beamed at Detective Donovan.

"You're the one who put through the call to 911."

"Actually my daughter, Jennifer, did—but at my request."

I piped up. "Actually the hotel operator made the call."

Detective Donovan's heavy eyebrows lowered as he glanced at me, then back to Mom. He referred to his notebook. "Mrs. . . . uh . . . Jakes, were you present when Porter Harmony died?"

"Oh, no," Mom said.

"But you said that you were aware he'd been murdered."

"Adam came rushing in, while Booth was getting ready to read Arnold's will, and told us."

Donovan's eyebrows met in a V as he tried to figure things out. "Reading his will . . . already? And you say that the deceased is named *Arnold* Harmony?"

"No," Mom said. "Adam distinctly said *Porter*."

"You were reading Porter Harmony's will *before* he died?"

"No, Arnold's will," Mom said. "That's why we're all here. Arnold invited us to a party to celebrate the reading of his will."

Donovan closed his eyes for an instant and took a deep breath that stretched his suit coat so tight, we could all see the lump below his left shoulder made by his holster and gun. "Let me get the facts straight," he said. "You were all having a party to celebrate Arnold Harmony's will. I take it that the celebration was because you were all mentioned in the will?"

"We have no idea," Mom said. "The will hasn't been read yet. We were waiting for Arnold and Porter to get here. It was his birthday party, too."

"Porter's?"

"Arnold's."

"You said that someone came in . . ."

"Adam. He's Arnold's employee."

I didn't want to listen to another round of questions and explanations, so I broke into the conversation. "Arnold Harmony is eighty-eight years old. Adam's a nurse who takes care of him and pushes his wheelchair."

"Thank you," Donovan said to me. "Maybe you'd like to explain what happened in this room when Adam came in and told you that Porter Harmony had been stabbed."

"Oh, good gracious!" Mom said. One hand went to her throat. "Is that how it happened?"

"Go ahead, Mr. Detective," Elsie said. "Give Madeline all the facts. Probably no one's told you yet, but she's here to help you solve the murder."

Chapter Six

Donovan took a step back, puzzled. "You're not with the San Antonio P.D., Mrs. Jakes. Who . . . ?"

"I'm not with anyone's police department," Mom answered. "I'm a mystery writer." She smiled. "Maybe you've read my mystery novels?"

"Sorry. I don't have much time for reading," Donovan said. He thought a moment. Then his lips pulled together as though he'd just said "pickle juice." "I suppose you're like that woman mystery writer character who used to be in a show on TV," he said. "My ex-wife used to watch her. Well, this is not TV, Mrs. Jakes. This is real life. I'll ask for plain, truthful answers when you're interrogated, and that's all I'll want. Is that understood?"

"We'll see about that!" Mabel cried out. "You aren't the first hardheaded cop our Madeline's come up against! Right, Madeline?"

Mom just smiled and murmured, "I'll be glad to help you in any way possible, Sergeant."

Donovan took a long appreciative look at Mom, then cleared his throat a couple of times before he said, "The best help you can give at this time is supplying answers to my questions. Do you know why Mr. Porter Harmony was staying in this hotel? The I.D. in his room lists an address in San Antonio."

Booth staggered to his feet, as though he had suddenly figured out what was going on. "I can give you the answers, Sergeant," he said. "I helped Mr. Arnold Harmony plan this gathering. My name is Booth Dockman, and I'm Mr. Harmony's attorney."

"Mr. Porter Harmony's attorney?"

"Yes and no. Primarily, I'm Mr. Arnold Harmony's attorney. I represent his company, Harmony Chocolates."

"Are there any other members of the immediate family?"

Solemnly Booth said, "Porter's stepson, Logan, is probably with his father's body right now."

"Not to my knowledge," Donovan said. "The scene of the crime had been secured by hotel personnel when I arrived. No one had been allowed inside."

"No one's there with poor Porter?" Elsie asked.

"Ma'am, the experts from our crime lab are on hand, going over every inch of the room. When they finish, the medical examiner's team will take over."

"Madeline!" Mabel whooped. "Shouldn't you hurry up and get in there right now so you can make sure they're doing everything right?"

At that moment Claudine threw open the door to the bathroom and stepped out. Her yellow hair lay damp and flat around her face. A major bad hair day. She glared at Detective Donovan and said, "I assume that you're with the police?"

"Yes, ma'am," he said. "I'm Sergeant Sam Donovan, homicide."

Claudine didn't look as though she planned to introduce herself, so Mom said, "This is Claudine Harmony, Sergeant Donovan. Arnold's wife."

Donovan referred to his notes and asked, "Not Porter's wife?"

"No," Alexa said. "Claudine is Porter's stepmother . . . like in Cinderella."

Donovan looked pained. "Is there a Mrs. Porter Harmony here?" he asked.

"Her name was Lydia Jane Harmony," Mom began.

Elsie interrupted, smiling. "Little Janie here is named after her," she said.

"I'm not Janie," I said. "I'm Jenny."

Mom broke in. "Lydia disappeared about fifteen years ago."

"Porter has repeatedly tried to find her," Elsie said.

Mom smiled at Donovan. "Your department should have that information in your records."

"Good going, Madeline," Mabel said, sounding like a cheerleader. "The detective didn't think about that, did he?"

Claudine held one hand to her forehead and swayed a little. "Sergeant Donovan," she said,

"I'm sure that Porter's murder will come as a terrible shock to my husband. He's eighty-eight and in frail health. I'd like to go to our suite and be with him."

"Very well, ma'am," Donovan said. "Just don't leave the hotel, please. I'll need to ask you some questions later." As Claudine walked out of the room, I twisted to peer through the open door, looking for Carlos. There were still a lot of people in the hallway, but Carlos was no longer there.

Donovan looked at Alexa. "Are you a member of the Harmony family?" he asked.

"I'm Alexa Blair," Alexa said. "I'm Arnold Harmony's personal business manager."

Gustave spoke up. "My name is Gustave Gunter, and I'm vice president of the Harmony Chocolates Company."

"So some of the people in this room are family, and some are employees of the Harmony company," Donovan said.

He walked around our grouping of chairs, stopping to write down names, addresses, and telephone numbers. Most of the employees were allowed to go home, as were a few relatives Donovan didn't seem to feel were necessary in his investigation. Elsie and Mabel were among those excused.

"Oh, darn," Elsie said. "I wanted to stick around and watch Madeline at work."

"It's like being on the set of a television show," Mabel added.

"Don't think we're going to check out of the hotel," Elsie said to Donovan. "We're going to be here when Madeline solves the crime."

As they left the room, I saw Mabel walk by the tray of chocolate mousse thingies and sneakily sweep a few of them into her big handbag. I hated to think what the handbag or the mousse thingies would look like by the time Mabel got to her room.

After most of the people there had departed, I glanced around to see who was left. It came down to Booth, Alexa, Gunter, Mom, and me.

"Mrs. Jakes, you and your daughter may leave," Donovan told her.

It was obvious that Mom didn't like being dismissed from a case Arnold's relatives expected her to solve, so I suppose she said the first thing that came into her mind. "I think you'll want to hear what I have to say." She stared pointedly at Alexa. "It may have a bearing on the murder."

"Mom," I whispered, "don't do this. You don't know why Porter was murdered." I felt kind of sick and kind of scared. Make-believe murders in mystery novels are okay to play around with. The mysteries are solved, and the bad guys get caught, but real-life murders are an entirely different thing. Someone killed Porter Harmony, and Mom didn't have a single idea why, but she was pretending that she did. Whoever murdered Porter could target Mom . . . or me . . . or both of us.

"The scene of an unsolved murder is not the

proper atmosphere for a young girl," Mom said, "so I may send Jennifer to stay with her grandmother."

"I'm not a young girl. I'm almost sixteen," I said.

"Sweetie, I'm your mother. I know what's best for you," she answered.

"Mom, in this case—"

Detective Donovan interrupted. "Please. Either leave and send Jennifer to her grandmother right this minute, or stay and send her after this meeting is over. I'd like to proceed."

"By all means," Mom told him. Then she said, as though she were talking to herself, *"Teapot."*

Alexa reacted, angrily hissing at Mom, "You don't know what you're talking about."

I whispered to Mom again, "Don't do this." I was afraid, from the look in Mom's eyes, that she was confusing herself with her fictional Audrey Downing again. What was I going to do? What could I do?

Mom smiled and patted my hand. "I have to help the detective, sweetie," she said, softly enough so the others couldn't hear. "For one thing, I want Porter's murder solved, and for another . . ." She took a deep breath, as though reality had actually touched her, and added, "You've heard what people have been saying about my skill as a mystery-writer detective. Like it or not, my reputation's on the line."

She didn't have to tell me. My stomach hurt, and my hands were sweaty. The only thing I could think of to do was try to get Mom out of this mess. Unfortunately not a single brilliant idea of how to do this came to me.

"Okay, Mrs. Jakes," Donovan said to Mom. "Stick around. I'll get to you later." He turned and spoke to Booth, who had sunk back into the chair behind the desk. "You're Arnold Harmony's attorney. Apparently his will was supposed to be read and signed here at your party tonight. I don't quite understand the significance of this. Would you mind filling me in?"

"Not at all," Booth said, "although I don't see how the reading of Arnold's will could have a bearing on Porter's murder."

"Don't try sorting things out. That's my job. Just give me the facts," Donovan said.

"Very well." Booth took a long, shuddering breath, clung to his briefcase, and said, "Arnold Harmony recently made some drastic changes in his will. He wanted this new will read in public where all his guests could see him sign it, just in case . . . well, in case later on anyone challenged the will in court, claiming that Arnold wasn't . . . um . . . thinking clearly. You understand."

"This public reading of a will before the person has died isn't exactly the normal way of doing things," Donovan said.

"This wasn't a normal execution of a will. The provisions in the will were planned to take place immediately after the reading and not after Arnold Harmony's death," Booth said.

"Arnold always has been vengeful," Gustave added.

Donovan turned to Gustave. "From the word you've just used, I assume that you know what is in this will."

Gustave shrugged. "I don't know the wording, but I can guess. When the will is made public, I'm sure we'll find that Arnold has not been fair with any of us."

"Had Arnold Harmony discussed the terms of his will with anyone earlier than tonight?" Donovan asked.

"No one but me, since I'm his attorney," Booth said. "He told me I would be the only one who would know the contents of the will until he chose to inform the others tonight."

"Do you have a copy of the will with you?"

"Yes. Right here."

Booth began to open his briefcase, but Mom spoke up. "Wait just a minute, please. Is the will pertinent to this murder investigation? And do you have a search warrant, Sergeant Donovan?"

Donovan, who had stepped up to the desk and already had a hand out, withdrew it. He said to Booth and not to Mom, "We don't know if we'll need a copy of the will. Just keep it available, please."

Mom smiled without a trace of smugness. I had to give her that.

Donovan walked over and sat beside Mom. The way he looked at her, I couldn't tell if he was interested in Mom or in what she had to tell him. "You said earlier you had some information that might help with the case," Donovan said. "Suppose you tell me what it is."

For just an instant Mom looked a little scared, so I blundered in.

"The information concerns someone in this room," I told Donovan. "I don't think Mom has the right to divulge it."

"I agree," Mom said. She sat up a little straighter.

Donovan began looking exasperated. "I'm not going to play guessing games with you, Mrs. Jakes."

"And I'm not going to give you the information I have at this moment," Mom answered. "Both parties are not present, so it would be unfair." She stared directly at Alexa.

This time Alexa didn't come up with a smart-aleck remark. She leaned against the hard back of her chair and said, "Madeline's right. Logan should be here."

"Because of *Teapot*," Mom said.

"I don't know how you discovered our code word," Alexa told her, "but surely you realize that it was no big deal. It doesn't have anything to do with Porter's murder."

Mom didn't answer, but Donovan unhooked a portable phone from his belt, punched in some numbers, and spoke to someone.

"Logan Harmony," he said. "Is he with his grandfather?"

There was a short pause before Donovan said, "He's not?" He looked at Mom. "Do you have a description for him?"

"Oh," Mom said. "Hmmm. He has a sort of a pouty . . ."

I didn't have a choice. I had to interrupt. "About five feet eleven inches, blond, early twenties. Jeans, white shirt, and navy blue blazer."

"Thanks," Donovan said. He repeated what I'd told him into the phone, then snapped, "Send an officer out to find him."

Chapter Seven

I got up, stretched, and slipped out of the Magnolia Suite while Mom, Alexa, and Sergeant Donovan were talking. I immediately headed for the bell stand on the lobby floor.

Carlos had just carried some bags inside for a couple of tourists, and his face lit up into a smile as he saw me.

"Hi, Jenny," he said. "How's Donovan's murder investigation going?"

Surprised, I asked, "Do you know Detective Donovan?"

"He's a good friend of the family," Carlos said. "He used to be my uncle's partner when my uncle was on the force—before he was shot in the leg and had to take disability." He grinned. "Has your mom got the case solved yet?"

"Not exactly," I said. "I—that is, Mom—wants to know if you've seen Logan Harmony anywhere around the hotel. Do you know what he looks like?"

"Sure," Carlos said. He nodded toward one

side of the lounge. There sat Logan, slumped in an overstuffed chair, an almost full glass of beer in his hand.

"Thanks," I said and elbowed my way through a group of brightly costumed tourists to the bank of house phones. I picked up the receiver and asked for the Magnolia Suite.

Booth answered, and I said, "I . . . uh . . . Mom sent me to the lounge to look for Logan. He's sitting right where she thought he'd be. Please tell Sergeant Donovan he can send someone down to get him."

Carlos was still with me. "Your mother's pretty good at detecting," he said. "Nobody working here wants the hotel to be the scene of a murder, but it's got everybody excited. They're watching and waiting to see what Madeline Jakes is going to do. It's like being in a television show."

"Have you ever seen someone who was murdered?" I asked.

"No," Carlos said. He looked at me curiously. "Have you?"

I shuddered and took a step closer to him. He put a hand on my shoulder, and his touch was strong and comforting.

"Once," I said. "It was before Mom's books began getting on the best-seller list. We didn't have much money, and we were living in a tiny apartment. There was a drive-by shooting on the sidewalk near our front door." I couldn't help shuddering again. "It was awful. I had nightmares for years. There's a big difference between make-believe, fictional murders and real murders."

"Yeah, I guess there would be," Carlos said. "It's not the kind of thing people think about."

"Unless it happens to someone they know," I said. I couldn't shake the feeling that Mom, who got make-believe and reality all mixed up, was deliberately walking into a dangerous situation. There was no way to stop her. There was little I could do, unless . . .

Two uniformed police officers stepped off the nearest elevator and passed us, heading for the lounge.

"I bet you're good at helping your mother solve crimes," Carlos said.

I looked up and beamed at Carlos, thankful for the idea he'd given me. "I'm going to try with this one," I said. "Just as her assistant, of course. I don't want her to get hurt in any way. Do you want to help me?"

"Sure," he said. "Just tell me what you want me to do."

"When do you get off work?"

"Ten-thirty, tonight, but I have tomorrow off." He pulled the stub of a pencil from one of his pockets and wrote on a scrap of paper someone had left by the phones. "Here's my phone number. I'll be back to see you tomorrow morning, but if you need me any time I'm not around, just call, and I'll come."

I took the paper, looked up into Carlos's big brown eyes, and melted. "Thanks," I said. "You're terrific."

"Carlos!" a voice from the bellmen's desk called.

"See you," Carlos said and trotted over to take care of a stack of luggage.

I stepped back as the police officers passed me, Logan between them. They got into one of the elevators, and I took the next. There was no telling what Mom might say or do. She needed me.

Gustave and Booth had left the Magnolia Suite by the time I returned. The uniformed police had vanished, too. The only people on hand were Alexa, Logan, Detective Donovan, and Mom.

Mom held out an arm and drew me protectively to her side. "Where were you, Jenny, my sweet?" she asked. "I was worried."

"I went down to the lobby for a minute," I said. "You were right. Logan was in the lounge."

Logan glared at me, but Mom looked pleased.

"Can we get down to business now?" Donovan asked Mom. "You said you had something to tell me. Something about a teapot?"

"Sergeant Donovan," I said, "don't you think the information would be more accurate if it came from the two people involved in *Teapot*, instead of a third party, who might not be impartial in telling the story? Alexa and Logan have the right to tell you in their own words what happened."

Alexa jumped in, a stubborn expression on her face, as though Mom had challenged her to a duel. "Jenny's right. I'll get a lawyer, if I have to, but I want to give you the facts my own way."

She pointed a finger at Mom. "I'm going to tell everything about *Teapot*. I won't leave anything out. So you keep out of it. No interrupting. No opinions. Understand?"

Mom nodded graciously, but Logan moaned and slid even farther down in his chair.

"We've got to explain, Logan," Alexa told him, "or they'll think *Teapot* had something to do with your father's murder, which is perfectly ridiculous."

Logan raised his head and managed to catch both Donovan and Mom in his angry glare. "I'm an orphan," he said. "Think about that for a minute. I'm an orphan, and you're not giving me a chance to mourn in peace."

Donovan didn't let that go by. "Mr. Dockman told me that you've been an orphan for fifteen years, that you and your stepfather weren't on very good terms, and that you rarely spent time together."

"So?" Logan snarled. "What has that got to do with anything?"

"Darling," Mom said to Logan, "maybe you'd like to come and visit us for a while. It would do you good to have caring loved ones around you."

"I haven't even seen you since I was ten, Madeline," Logan said. "When did you become a caring loved one?"

"Right now," Mom answered. *"Mi casa es su casa."* She held out her arms, and I knew she meant it. Mom is very tenderhearted.

"Let's stick to the subject," Donovan said. He

looked at Alexa. "Will you please begin, Miss Blair?"

"Over the years Logan has been given quite a few shares in Harmony Chocolates," Alexa said. "Through my contacts as Arnold's personal business manager, I discovered an opportunity for Logan to make a great deal of money selling his shares to an up-and-coming beverage company that wants to expand in this part of the country. Naturally we wanted to keep Logan's activities secret, so we used the code name *Teapot* for all our communications and transactions."

"But the project fell through," Mom said.

I interrupted. "Let Alexa tell why, Mom."

"Logan's shares weren't as free and clear as we had thought," Alexa said.

"And your part in this?" Mom asked.

"I told you to stay out. I'd tell it my way," Alexa snapped. She twisted so that her back was half turned to Mom and she was facing Sergeant Donovan. "Logan was to receive a well-paid position with the beverage company, and I was to be his assistant—also well paid."

"More so than as Cousin Arnold's personal business manager?" Mom asked.

"Make her stop," Alexa said to Donovan. "She has no right butting in."

"I was about to ask you the same question," Donovan said to Alexa. "Will you please answer it?"

"Yes," Alexa mumbled. "It was more money."

"How did Arnold Harmony feel about the

plan you and Logan had made for his Harmony Chocolates shares?"

"He doesn't know about it," Alexa said. Her heavy makeup was getting old and orange, and she began to resemble a drooping Halloween pumpkin mask. "Look, we gave it a shot, but it's over. It's done with. Arnold doesn't need to know, does he?"

Donovan didn't answer her question. Instead he asked, "Did Porter Harmony know?"

"No. I told you, no one knew besides Logan and me."

Mom cleared her throat, and Alexa turned to glower at her. "And you," she said. "It was kept so secret. How could you possibly figure it out?"

Mom just sat there looking enigmatic. How cool can you get?

Donovan asked Logan, "Would you like to add something to what Miss Blair told us?"

Logan shook his head. "No. She said it all."

Donovan got to his feet. Automatically the rest of us stood, too. "Miss Blair, Mr. Harmony, you may be excused," he said. "Mrs. Jakes, I suppose you want to get your daughter on a late flight."

As the others left the room, Donovan moved a little closer to Mom. "Want to tell me where you got the information?" he asked.

Mom's lips parted, but when nothing came out I said, "Sergeant Donovan, Madeline Jakes is a writer. She has the constitutional right to protect her sources."

Mom smiled at Donovan, and his face seemed to mellow. He didn't look nearly as tough. "Just tell me this," he said. "Was Miss Blair right? Or does this projected stock sale have a bearing on Porter Harmony's murder?"

"I haven't heard enough details about the murder to be positive," Mom said, "but at this moment I think we can rule out the *Teapot* connection."

Donovan made a few notes in his book. Mom watched him and said, "If I knew more about the murder . . ."

"I'm going to the scene of the crime," Donovan said. "There are some things I need to check out. If you'd like, after you see your daughter off, you can join me there."

"Please, Mom," I said. "I don't want to visit Grandma. I want to stay with you. Maybe I can even help you."

Mom smiled lovingly at me, then glanced at Donovan, who was walking toward the doorway. "Wait for me, Sergeant," she said. "Jennifer is going to stay."

"Fine," Donovan said. "I'll fill you in with some of the facts in the case along the way." He walked out of the room.

"Mom," I said, "I'll have to change the flight reservation we have for Sunday evening."

"Oh," Mom said. "I guess we will have to do something about that."

We? "I'll take care of it. Do you want openended?"

"I guess so," Mom said, making sure her voice

62

was low enough so that Donovan wouldn't hear. "I don't know exactly when I'll wind up this case."

She hurried to join Donovan, and I tagged after, picking up scraps of the conversation. Donovan said, "He was stabbed with the fruit knife that came along with a tray of fruit and cheese from the hotel's gift shop."

"Oh, dear," Mom said.

I took a couple of quick steps to catch up. "Who sent the fruit and cheese tray?" I asked.

Donovan looked at me as though surprised I was still there. "Alexa Blair. She told me it was part of her job to send trays to Arnold Harmony's guests."

"We didn't get one," I said.

"The world is filled with oversights, my sweet," Mom said. "The last thing in the world we need to think about now is a fruit and cheese tray." She said to Donovan, "Before we joined the reception, we spoke with Porter. He told me he was glad we had come because he wanted to talk to me."

"About what?"

"I don't know. He felt it was important to speak in private. We were supposed to have our talk tonight, after the will was read."

"You have no idea what he wanted to talk about?" Donovan asked.

"No, I don't," Mom said.

As we reached the elevators, Donovan said, "Mrs. Jakes—"

"Please call me Madeline."

"All right. Madeline." The elevator bell dinged, or we might have stood there an hour while he smiled at Mom. The bell seemed to remind Donovan what he'd had in mind, because he said, "I can't allow your daughter to come with us to the crime scene. I don't think you'll want her there, either. I was informed that the hallway outside is swarming with newspaper and television crews."

I wasn't eager to see the crime scene, either, but I hated to leave Mom alone with an active imagination, a desire to solve a real crime, and a good-looking cop.

"It's really late," Mom said. "Sweetie, why don't you go back to the room? You have your key, don't you?"

I fumbled inside my handbag, then shook my head. "I'm sure I put the key in here," I answered, "but now I can't find it." During the evening I'd laid my handbag down on chairs or tables or wherever, but I hadn't thought much about it. I carried less than five dollars, so there wasn't anything in the bag that anyone would want.

Mom reached into her bag and handed me the plastic card that served as a key. "You'll probably find that you left your key in the room," she said.

Donovan impatiently held the elevator door open. "I haven't got time to wait, Madeline," he told her.

"All right, Sam," she answered. She blew me a kiss.

"Are you sure you'll be okay?" I asked Mom, but the elevator doors were already closing.

I was in no mood to go to bed or even watch television, so I took the next elevator down to look for Carlos.

"He's off duty," the bell captain told me, so I wandered around, examining the lobby and looking in the windows of the closed gift shops.

That was no fun, so reluctantly I got on an elevator and headed for the eighth floor. I didn't know when Mom would be back, but maybe there was a good movie to watch.

As I opened the door, I flipped on the light in the entryway and saw that the pair of queen-sized beds had been turned down, with wrapped chocolate mints on the fluffed pillows. It took only five minutes to eat both mints, pull the airline tickets out of my travel bag in the minicloset, phone the airlines, and put the tickets away again.

Music floated up from the river below, along with a burst of laughter, and I smiled. Eager to get a look at the twinkling lights and the dark water and the late party goers, I opened the sliding glass door and stepped out onto the balcony.

The door was silent as it slid shut behind me. It wasn't until I heard a click as it shut and locked that I realized what had happened. I whirled around, yelling, "Hey!" and banged on the glass door, but the drapes had been closed. I'd surprised someone in our room—someone who had probably jumped into the bathroom to hide when I came in.

Who was it? Why was this person in our room? And how long was I going to be stuck out here on this balcony?

Chapter Eight

I leaned over the railing to see if there was anyone around who could help me. A voice suddenly spoke from above, startling me so much
that I nearly went over the side.

"Janie! What do you think you're doing hanging over that railing?"

"Mabel?" I asked and turned to peer upward.

Both Elsie and Mabel stared down at me from
a nearby balcony on the tenth floor.

"Be a good girl. Go inside and stop playing out
on the balcony," Elsie said.

"I locked myself out," I told them, deciding
not to tell what had really happened. "Will
you call the front desk and ask them to send
someone to open the door?" I gave them my
room number.

"You call them, Elsie," Mabel said. "I'm going
to wait right here until Janie goes inside so I can
make sure she doesn't keep doing silly things like
leaning over the railing."

"Good idea," Elsie said. She disappeared from

view, and I sighed with relief that these nosy sisters had seen me out here.

It seemed like hours, but according to my watch, it took only a few minutes before the drapes were drawn back and the sliding glass door was opened.

A short, plump woman wearing a badge labeled HOUSEKEEPING looked at me with a puzzled expression on her face. "How did you get out there with the door locked and the drapes closed?" she asked.

"I wish I knew," I said. "Thanks for rescuing me."

"Rescuing?" Her eyes widened.

I shrugged. "All I know is that somebody locked the door while I was out on the balcony."

"You didn't see who it was?"

"No. Whoever did it closed the drapes."

Quickly she said, "Well, it's a sure thing that nobody in housekeeping did it. They turned down the beds in here half an hour ago, and there's no reason anyone would come back." She paused, then said questioningly, "Unless you asked for a special service."

"The only special service was that you unlock the sliding door and let me inside, which you just did." I thanked her again, and she left.

I took the elevator to the fourth floor, where I found Mom and Donovan in the hallway outside the crime scene. Thank goodness they weren't still inside the room and I didn't have to look at anything I didn't want to see. And thank goodness the media people had left.

"Jenny?" Mom asked. "I thought you'd be curled up with a good movie by now."

"Oh, Mom," I said and hugged her. The minute her arms were around me the scary part of being locked out hit me. It took a few minutes before I could calm down enough to tell Mom and Donovan what had happened, and when I did, I remembered every detail. "Someone must have hid in the bathroom when I came in," I said.

Mom frowned. "There's something I don't understand. When you walked out on the balcony, the person could have slipped out of the bathroom and out of the room, and you wouldn't have known the difference. But the person took the chance of being seen by locking you out on the balcony. Why?"

There was only one reason I could think of. "Because the person hadn't finished what he was doing, like . . . uh . . . searching the room?"

"Guesses aren't good enough," Donovan said. "Let's take a look."

As we got off the elevator, there was Carlos, out of uniform, in jeans and a T-shirt. "Hi, Jenny," he said. "I came by to see if you'd like to get ice cream."

"Isn't this a little late?" Mom asked, but I interrupted.

"It's not that late," I said. "Not on a Fiesta weekend. Please stay, Carlos. I'd like to go with you to get some ice cream." I introduced Carlos to Mom and Donovan.

"Carlos and I have been friends from way

back," Donovan said. "How's the job going, Carlos?"

"Fine, sir," Carlos said. "I'm off duty now, so I'm available to help with the murder investigation."

Donovan shook his head. "Nope. I'm conducting an official investigation, and the parties on site should be kept to a minimum."

"Hey, Donovan, I wasn't going to make it a party." Carlos's eyes twinkled.

I gave Donovan a look that I hoped he'd understand and said, "I don't think anyone here really means to interfere with anyone else's social life, do they?"

Before Donovan could answer, Mom asked him, "I assume that you know Carlos well?"

Donovan had to smile and said, "Carlos is okay. He's a good kid. His uncle was the best partner I ever had."

Mom smiled a welcome to Carlos, walked down the hall to our room, and opened the door.

Donovan was first inside the room, but Mom and I stretched to look around him.

"Nothing looks out of place," Mom said. She pointed to the top of the chest of drawers. "Look, Jenny," Mom said. "There's your key, just where you left—"

Quickly I said, "Mom, I know you're going to remind Detective Donovan to take the key in for fingerprints. Flat plastic will hold prints, unless the perpetrator wore gloves." I felt as though Uncle Bill's words were coming out of my mouth, but I went on. "You probably guessed already that someone took the key out of my handbag during the evening. He—or she—must have used it to enter the room."

"Yes, of course," Mom said. I could hear excitement in her voice, as though she were the one who'd just thought of it. "Your key's on the chest of drawers, and everything's in place, so the person who did this . . ."

She drifted to a puzzled stop, so I finished her sentence. "The person who did this probably thought you had sent me to Grandma's and they'd have more time for what they wanted to do. Mom, you're so right."

"Exactly what do you think they wanted to do?" Mom asked.

I shrugged. "Let's look in the drawers and see if anyone went through our things."

We both checked, but as far as we could tell, nothing had been disturbed.

"How about the bathroom?" I asked. "The person must have been hiding in there. Maybe there's a clue in the bathroom."

I started toward the bathroom, but Donovan grabbed my arm. "*I'll* check it out," he said. From the strange look on his face I was sure he'd thought of something we hadn't.

He reappeared in less than a minute and glanced at the table on the right side of the bed. "Your clock radio," he said.

Mom and I looked, and she said, "It's gone. I hadn't noticed."

"No, and you probably wouldn't have. It was on, with the volume turned so low no one could hear it, and it was wired to . . . let's just say that if you tried to wash your hands you would have received an electrical shock—probably not fatal but very unpleasant."

I gasped. "Mom!"

Detective Donovan wrapped the little radio in a plastic hotel laundry bag he took from the closet.

"Many people are in and out of these rooms each day—guests, maids, waiters from room service, repairmen, you name it," Donovan said. "So dusting the room for fingerprints would be useless. However, we can check the radio and key card for prints."

"If I were the culprit, I'd have worn gloves in handling the radio and wiped the plastic key card free of prints," I told Donovan.

He nodded. "You're probably right, but it's worth a try. I'll send them to the lab."

"Does Jenny have to stick around?" Carlos asked Mom. "We could go down to the river, and walk around with the people in costume, and eat ice cream."

Mom was pale, and her fingers trembled against my arm. "Oh, Carlos," she said, "I know you're a perfectly lovely person, and under normal circumstances I'd be glad to let Jenny go down to the Riverwalk with you. But after what happened in this room, I can't bear to let her out of my sight."

She looked at me, rather than at Carlos. "You understand, don't you, sweetie?"

"Sure," Carlos answered.

"I'm the only one she calls *sweetie*," I explained.

"There's a coffee shop on the lobby level of the hotel that's open twenty-four hours a day," Mom said. "I'm sure they serve ice cream. Why don't we all go down there?"

"I'm on duty. I have to work," Donovan said.

"You can take time for one cup of coffee," Mom said. "Cops and coffee. That's standard procedure."

In her mystery novels, I thought.

"And we can talk about some of the questions that are puzzling us."

"Like what?" Donovan asked.

Mom batted her eyes as though signaling in an idea—any idea. So I said, "Mom, you were wondering awhile ago about those fruit and cheese trays for Arnold's guests. Who got them and who didn't, who placed the order, when they were delivered . . . all that stuff."

"So I was," Mom said. She rested her fingertips on Donovan's arm. "We should discuss these points, shouldn't we, Sam?"

Sam Donovan gave in without much of a fight. "Solving this crime is *my* job, not yours," he said, "but I could use a cup of coffee."

We waited while Donovan telephoned for someone to meet him and pick up the radio and key. Then we headed for the coffee shop.

Mom and Donovan took a table near the entrance, while Carlos and I settled down near the back of the room, as far away as we could get. Mom could still keep an eye on me, since I was facing her, but I didn't feel as if she were right on top of us.

"I'm sorry about all of this," I said to Carlos. "If you want to leave, I'll understand."

"You're kidding," Carlos said. "You're the most interesting person I've ever met."

"You mean my mother is the most interesting person."

"No, I mean you. A little while ago I began to figure something out. You—"

A waitress came up with menus and hung around while we read them and ordered. I asked for a root beer float, and Carlos ordered the Fiesta special, which was made of four scoops of ice cream, four toppings, whipped cream, nuts, and little Fiesta flags sprouting out of the top.

"I always wanted to try one of those," Carlos said after the waitress had left, "but I couldn't because I'm an employee and I'm not allowed to eat here."

I stared at him, surprised. "Nobody's thrown you out."

He grinned. "That's because I'm with you. Next time I'm on duty everyone's going to grill me about what I found out and what your mother's doing to solve the crime, and what you're like and all that."

"Oh? Just what am I like?" I asked.

"You're a fraud," Carlos answered.

I jumped. "I'm a what?"

"A fraud," he said. "I was listening up there in the room. It wasn't your mother having all those brainstorm ideas about how the crime was committed and how to solve it. Those ideas were *yours*."

"Oh, c'mon," I said. "Mom's the mystery writer, not me."

"I bet you read mysteries."

"Well, yes. I like to read mysteries."

"And I could tell that you know something about how the police work, aside from what you read in the books."

I smiled at him. "You're a good detective your-self. Mom's brother—my uncle Bill Harrison—is a homicide detective in the Houston Police De-partment. I love to talk to him about his cases and what he does. He answers a lot of questions for Mom and makes sure the police procedures in her stories are right."

"Do you want to be a mystery writer, like your mother, someday?"

"No," I said. "But I've thought about being a policewoman, or a private investigator. How about you? What do you want to be?"

"A journalist," Carlos answered.

"Like your columnist friend?"

"No. I'd hate writing a column—especially about famous people and all the parties they go to. What I want to be is a reporter, writing the big stories, in on all the exciting stuff."

The waitress came with our order, and we be-gan to pig out. But first Carlos wiped the whipped cream from the bottom of the cluster of Fiesta flags and gave them to me. It would have been a really tender moment, except that Mom was watching.

"Does your mother know how much help you give her when she solves crimes?" Carlos asked.

I groaned. "You said that the people who work with you want to hear everything we talked about," I said. "Please don't tell them what you think about how Mom solves mysteries. It would ruin her reputation."

"I'm not going to tell them a thing," Carlos said.

"That newspaper columnist who pays you for information," I said. "You especially can't tell him. Some things have to be secret."

Carlos laid one hand over his heart. "I respect your secrets," he said, "even the ones you don't tell me, which I'm clever enough to figure out."

I had to laugh. "I love my mother very much, even though I don't always understand her and she drives me crazy," I admitted to Carlos.

After I said the words, they didn't seem to make much sense, but Carlos nodded solemnly, as if he understood. My left hand was resting on the table, and Carlos placed his right hand over it. "Let me be with you while you solve the crime," he said. "We can both help your mother."

"It's not a game," I told him. "Tonight I was scared."

Carlos's eyes softened. "I'm sorry, Jenny."

I gulped, and suddenly my hand turned upward, so my fingers were intertwined with his. "Being around me may not be safe," I told him.

"It may be safer, with two of us together."

Two of us together. I liked that. "And Mom," I said.

"And Mom," Carlos echoed with a grin. He turned so that he could look back at Mom, but she and Donovan had left their table and were standing at the cash register. Mom's back was toward us.

Before I knew what was happening, Carlos had leaned across the table and kissed me lightly on my lips. The kiss was cool and sweet with vanilla and chocolate and just a hint of whipped cream. *Forget about murder*, I thought.

But I didn't have a chance.

Mom swept up and leaned over the table, speaking low. "Jenny," she said, "something very upsetting has happened. You must come with us. Now. Carlos may come, too, if he wishes. But act calm and collected. We all must pretend that nothing is wrong."

Chapter Nine

It wasn't until we reached the fourth floor and Donovan had knocked at the door of suite 487 that Mom explained. Claudine and a Dr. Miles had been with Arnold when he was told about Porter's murder. Arnold became so upset he had to be sedated.

"That figures," I began. "Porter was his son."

Claudine opened the door, and Donovan angrily barged into the room, nearly pushing her aside. "You were instructed to page me. I asked to be here when Mr. Arnold Harmony was told about the death of his son."

Claudine shrugged, and I could see defiance in her eyes. She'd never had any intention of obeying Donovan's request. "When Arnold awoke from his nap, he asked what time it was," she said. "Then he asked where Porter was and why he hadn't awakened him so that the final stage of the party could take place. Arnold insisted on an answer. Dr. Miles was here, so I told Arnold what had happened to Porter. As you can see, we had to sedate Arnold."

"It was important that I talk to Mr. Harmony," Donovan said. He glared at the doctor, who looked as though he'd like to be anywhere but there.

"H-His wife thought it would be wise to sedate him," Dr. Miles stammered.

"What did Arnold say when you told him about Porter?" I asked Claudine.

"Nothing anyone could understand," Claudine said. "He babbled a bit, but his words were garbled."

"Except . . . ," Dr. Miles said timidly.

"Except what?" Mom asked.

"I told you," Claudine insisted, her voice rising. "He didn't say anything that could be understood."

Donovan stepped between Claudine and Dr. Miles. "What did *you* hear Mr. Harmony say, Dr. Miles?"

"Well, I may . . . uh . . . be wrong. . . ."

"Let me decide that," Donovan said. "Tell me what you heard."

Dr. Miles took a shuddering breath. I noticed that he didn't look in Claudine's direction. "I thought I heard Mr. Harmony say, 'Porter was right. I should have listened.' "

As Donovan went on talking with both the doctor and Claudine and taking notes, I pulled Mom aside. "Everyone thinks Porter's murder must have had something to do with Arnold's will."

"It did, my sweet," Mom told me. "Why else would it have happened when it did?"

"Mom, you've probably already figured out that Porter could have been murdered because he was going to tell his father something bad about someone mentioned in his will."

Mom jumped on that idea. "It's logical."

"Okay. So let's say that Porter knew something bad about someone and was going to tell his father. But . . . what if he were murdered around this reading-of-the-will party just to throw the police off the track? To make them think the murder had something to do with the will, when it didn't? The murderer could be real tricky, Mom."

"Hmmm," Mom said. Her brain seemed to hum as it moved into gear. "We've got two very distinct possibilities to consider."

"Then it's time for the next step," I said.

"Which is?"

"You know. Finding out everything we can about Porter Harmony and why he told you, 'There've been too many parties. Something must be done.'"

"Of course," Mom said. "Something in Porter's life must be the key. We'll need to check out his work, his social life, his hobbies—"

As Donovan joined us, tucking his notebook and pen back into his pocket, Mom said, "Sam, I feel that the key to what has happened lies in Porter Harmony's notes, files, or maybe even his social calendar—something in which Porter would record or store information."

"Why?" Donovan asked.

Mom blinked just once. Then she brought out that special enigmatic smile and actually looked as though she knew something important that no one else could know. "Trust me," she said.

A knock on the door, the creak, and the clatter of the room service breakfast cart awoke me the next morning. Mom signed the bill and ushered the waiter out before she called gently, "Wake up. Breakfast has arrived, Jennifer, my sweet."

The moment Mom opened the drapes, I rubbed my eyes against the blast of sunlight that slammed into the room.

"What time is it?" I mumbled as I crawled out of bed.

"Nearly seven," Mom replied. "We've got work to do. Eat up."

I reached for the newspaper that was neatly folded on the breakfast tray. It was the fat Sunday *San Antonio Light*. The front-page lead story was about Arnold's birthday party and Porter's murder. The reading of Arnold's will was not mentioned. I felt pretty sure the police hadn't given out that information.

There was also a sidebar about Madeline Jakes, the mystery-writer detective, with a photo of Mom and Donovan at the scene of the crime. I tossed the paper to the nearest bed. With all this publicity about what Mom was supposed to be able to do, she'd *have* to solve this murder.

I was so worried I thought I'd never be able to

81

eat again, but Mom lifted the round silver lid that covered my plate, and the wonderful spicy fragrance of picante sauce made my mouth water. "Ummm, huevos rancheros," I said. Mom had already seated herself, so I pulled a chair up to the table, picked up a fork, and began to demolish the eggs on my plate.

As we ate, Mom said that she'd already checked on Arnold's condition and was told that he was still sleeping peacefully.

"Has he talked to Detective Donovan yet?" I asked.

"No," Mom said. "He hasn't awakened to talk to anyone."

"Is there any way we can find out what's in the new will that Arnold was going to sign, and compare it to the old will?" I asked.

"I suppose so," Mom answered, "if Booth cooperates." She thought a moment and sighed. "I may have been too defensive last night when I brought up the need for a search warrant. I was just . . . well, it was something Audrey Downing would have done."

"Mom, stay real," I said. "You are *not*—repeat *not*—Audrey Downing." I could hear the exasperation in my voice. I was sorry for it because Mom bristled.

"Audrey doesn't make wrong moves. She evaluates a situation and knows where she's going."

"Audrey doesn't, Mom. *You* do. Audrey's just a fictional character. You're the writer. You decide what Audrey should or shouldn't do."

"And I check everything with Bill," Mom

said. "When I send a manuscript to my editor, I know the police procedure is entirely correct."

This argument was going nowhere. "It's okay, Mom," I said. "You were standing up for Arnold's constitutional rights. There's nothing wrong with that. Now, though, it would be a good idea to see what Arnold wanted in both wills. It would show who was being left out and who had been added."

Mom tapped her knife on the edge of the tray. "But last night you said that Porter's murder might have nothing to do with the will. That the reading of Arnold's new will might have been used to cover up the reason for Porter's murder."

"It could have happened that way," I said. "In any case, differences in the two wills might give us a clue to the identity of the murderer."

The telephone rang, and I jumped, but Mom was calm and answered it. She smiled, and her voice softened. I knew it was Donovan.

"Right away," Mom finally said and hung up. "Sam's at the scene of the crime," she said. "Last night he promised to let me take a look for possible clues."

"Porter's body isn't still there, is it?" I couldn't help shuddering.

"Of course not," Mom answered. She took a gulp of coffee. "If you want to come with me, hurry and get ready."

As we stepped off the elevator, the nearby door to the stairway flew open and Carlos staggered out, gasping for breath. A camera dangled on a cord around his neck. "There was no answer

83

at your room. The housekeeper said you'd just left. I thought you'd be here," he managed to say.

My heart gave a thump. I was surprised how glad I was to see Carlos.

"Good morning, Carlos," Mom said, smiling from behind a swirl of her peach chiffon scarf. "I'm so happy that you joined us." She really was, too. I knew Mom's thinking. I'll be easier to keep in sight if Carlos is on hand, too.

When we arrived at the scene of the crime, Detective Sam Donovan wasn't alone. Booth was there, along with Gustave and Alexa. The living room was gorgeous, in shades of blue and green with lots of beautifully polished tables, china ornaments, and crystal lamps, but I didn't spend more than five seconds admiring the room.

As Mom had promised, Porter's body had been taken away, but there were still chalk marks on the floor where the detectives had drawn a line around the body, and there were some dark stains in the mottled pattern of the carpet that couldn't be anything else but blood. I tried not to look at them and stuck close to Mom. The suite was on the same side of the hotel as our room. The large sliding glass doors, which led to another balcony, framed a vista of sunshine and flowers—a very different world from that inside this room.

Carlos looked at the carpet stains and moved closer to me. "Mrs. Jakes, could I take your picture with Jenny—right here—wow!—at the scene of the crime?" Carlos asked.

"No way!" I said.

Mom was more polite. "Not here, dear," she answered. "Maybe when we leave. How about outside the hotel in the patio?"

Booth, Gustave, and Alexa silently watched us as we walked across the room to join them.

"What is *she* doing here?" Alexa demanded of Donovan.

"Mrs. Jakes is here to give me some assistance," Donovan answered. He said to Mom, "I'm glad you could come, Madeline. I've received the lab reports, and Mr. Dockman was just explaining to me why his fingerprints were on a glass in this suite."

Booth fidgeted nervously. "I didn't deny I was here. I came to see Porter soon after we were served our salads at dinner last night. I'll be quite open with you. I asked him if he could influence his father to cancel the public reading and signing of his will. I felt the entire proceedings were . . . inappropriate."

"Why were your fingerprints on the glass?" Mom asked.

"I was thirsty. There had been too much salt in the salad dressing. I asked for some water."

Donovan made another note, then asked, "How did Porter Harmony respond to your proposal?"

"He told me that his father's mind was made up, and he wouldn't change it." Booth shook his head and looked sorrowful. "There never was a good relationship between the two of them. No affection, none of the father-and-son bond. Arnold only seemed to care about his chocolate company. At least, on the whole, he was pleased that Porter ran it efficiently."

"We were told that there was no particular affection between Porter and his son, Logan, either," Mom added.

"Stepson," Alexa insisted.

Donovan asked Booth, "How long were you in Porter Harmony's room?"

"Only a few minutes," Booth said. "There was a knock on the door, and I answered it. Alexa came into the room, so I left."

"Alexa Blair? You're Mr. Arnold Harmony's business manager?"

Booth interrupted. "That's *personal* business manager. Alexa had nothing to do with the operation of the Harmony Chocolates Company. Basically her job consists of managing Arnold's contributions to various charities—and attending parties, balls, fund-raisers . . ."

Alexa glowered at Booth. "Don't sound so condescending. It's a difficult job attending all those parties, not just here in San Antonio, but in Dallas, Houston, Los Angeles, New York, Washington, D.C. . . . once, even in London. At times the schedule can be exhausting."

Donovan didn't seem impressed. He asked, "Why did you visit Mr. Porter Harmony in his suite last night?"

"I had a perfectly good reason," Alexa answered. She glanced in Gustave's direction. "I wanted to warn Porter that Gustave was up to no good. He was sure that Arnold was going to double-cross him, so Gustave planned to pull his double cross first. Gustave had told Porter that he wanted Arnold to admit in writing that the recipe that made Harmony Chocolates famous really belonged to Gustave until Arnold stole it from him."

Gustave's face was so white, he looked as if he might faint. "Now just a minute!" he said. Gustave held on to the back of a chair, and the color began to come back into his face. "Detective Donovan," he said, "Alexa has made the situation sound much worse than it was."

"Alexa, how did you know about this?" Mom asked.

"I . . . I overheard part of the conversation," Alexa said.

Donovan asked Gustave, "Did you have a discussion of this nature with Mr. Dockman?"

"Yes, I did. Last night. Just before dinner was served."

"And with Porter Harmony?"

"Yes. At the same time. And it's true that Arnold Harmony stole my recipe. Many years ago, when I was a very young man, we went into partnership and founded the candy company. Arnold brought the financial backing, and I brought the recipe to the partnership. I thought we'd be sharing equally, and I trusted Arnold, so I didn't read everything in the contract before signing it." He paused and gave a heartbreaking sigh. "I was a fool to have been so trusting. That recipe belonged to my grandmother, and Arnold took all rights to it. I-I'd better tell you. I threatened to sue Arnold. I told him this myself."

"Was the attorney who drew up the contract aware that the recipe belonged to you?" Donovan asked.

"Yes! He was just as crooked as Arnold Harmony!" Gustave turned and pointed a finger at Booth's chest. "The attorney was Booth Dockman's father!"

"This is ridiculous," Booth said. He tried to stay cool, but his cheeks and nose turned red. I could see his hands tremble.

Donovan asked, "Mr. Dockman, did your father ever discuss this with you?"

"No, because it wasn't important. It's just Gustave's story, and he could claim anything, couldn't he? There's no way he could prove that's his recipe."

Gustave was angry now. "You won't get the truth from Booth. For years he's been getting a fat retainer from Arnold as the company's attorney. Of course he'd be on Arnold's side."

Donovan turned to Claudine. "Mrs. Harmony, has your husband ever discussed Mr. Gunter's claim with you?"

Claudine sneered at Gustave. "Good gracious, no," she said. "When the company was established, I was a mere child. I've only been married to Arnold for the past seven years, and we *never* talked business."

"Did you talk business with Porter Harmony?"

"No. In fact, I rarely saw Porter."

88

"How about yesterday evening, here in Porter's suite?"

"I was not here," Claudine answered. "I had nothing to discuss with Porter, business or otherwise."

"Mom," I whispered, "what was Porter's job with Harmony Chocolates?"

She immediately asked Booth the same question.

"Porter essentially ran Harmony Chocolates," Booth said. "Of course, every major decision had to go through Arnold for his approval."

"Hmmm," Mom said. "Arnold wouldn't relinquish the power. Is that it?"

"I'm not at liberty to say."

Donovan spoke to Booth. "Do you know of any recent conflicts between Porter and his father?"

Alexa snickered and answered before Booth could open his mouth. "There were always conflicts. Porter wanted to make changes in advertising and marketing the chocolates. Arnold wouldn't allow any changes. Porter wanted to streamline accounting. Arnold said the old system was good enough for him."

"Wasn't the company computerized?" I asked in surprise.

Booth looked surprised. "Of course, it was," he said, "but that's neither here nor there."

"I know Mom doesn't agree with you," I said. "Probably Detective Donovan has asked for a search warrant already."

Mom rested her fingertips on Donovan's arm

and looked into his eyes. "And one that will cover both wills," she said.

"The warrant for the wills has already been requested," Donovan said. He pulled out his phone, walked to a corner of the room, and made a call.

Booth puffed up and blustered. "I don't see the need for any of this."

"Why, of course you do, darling," Mom said. "Porter had something he wanted to talk about. He may have told his father, or he may not. In either case, we have to discover what it was. If it's something that had to do with the chocolate company and its operations, then it's important to go through Porter's computer files."

Mom gracefully leaned against a table and twined her fingers in the scarf that draped her shoulders. A faraway look came into her eyes. "I've done quite a bit of research on computers for a mystery novel I've just completed. I discovered that a computer can tell us many things through what it contains . . . or what it's missing," Mom said, a touch of mystery creeping through her words. "Hypothetically let's say that there's always the possibility of computer fraud. If there's evidence, the computer will give it to us. It won't be hard to find it."

I groaned, realizing that Mom was into her character Audrey's last plot, even quoting some of her dialogue. Computer fraud was the latest fad in murder mysteries, so of course, Mom's imagination was into computer crime. I didn't want to have to deal with Audrey Downing. I wanted Mom to be Mom.

"The trick is knowing what to look for," Mom said in Audrey's words. She smiled at Booth. "And I do."

"Y-You kn-know?" he stammered, unwittingly reciting the story's next line of dialogue.

"I know," Mom-Audrey said.

I opened my mouth to set things straight, but Booth took a step forward. He swayed, although he tried to steady himself by clutching the edge of a desk. His face turned that gross cheesy color again.

"There's no need to search the company's computers, Madeline, since you know what happened," Booth said. "I don't understand why you pretended at first that you didn't know, because Porter must have told you. Otherwise, how could you have found out?"

Donovan's voice was low as he spoke into Mom's left ear. "How *did* you know? *What* do you know? What haven't you told me?"

Mom, having nothing to say, didn't answer. Her smile was enough to fluster Booth and puzzle Donovan even more.

"Granted, it was a bad mistake," Booth blurted out, "but we thought we had handled it as well as could be expected." He stared at Mom as though she were a witch. "It *was* Porter who told you, wasn't it? Or else how in the world could you possibly have known about it?"

Chapter Ten

Donovan hooked his cellular telephone on to his belt. He gripped Booth's arm and steadied him into the nearest chair. "Get him some water," he said to Gustave.

He waited until Booth had taken some deep breaths and choked down some sips of water before he said, "Let's hear what you have to say about the computer fraud."

"Extortion. Computer extortion," Booth corrected. He looked up at Mom with desperate eyes. "Madeline may as well tell you about it. I . . . I don't think I'm up to it."

Mom looked at me for an answer. Carlos was watching me, too, waiting to hear what I'd have to say. I took a deep breath and tried to sound stern. "That won't cut it, Mr. Dockman," I said. "Detective Donovan needs to hear your story in your own words."

"But it's not my story!" Booth exclaimed. "Besides, I'd rather that the guilty party were here.

Considering the circumstances, I don't want to talk behind his back."

Only one of the family members was missing and unaccounted for, so I took the chance. "Mom, do you want to send for Logan?" I asked.

"I wish you would," Booth said.

Mom nodded regally at Donovan. "If you please," she said.

"I-I'd just as soon he didn't get the idea that I had anything to do with this," Booth added.

Donovan picked up the house phone and asked for Logan's room. He barked at him that he had exactly ten minutes to get himself out of bed and put in an appearance.

During that ten minutes no one talked much. Alexa, Booth, and Gustave kept sneaking curious looks at Mom, and I wondered if they were somewhat afraid of her.

Carlos winked at me, his lips upturned as though we shared a joke. I frowned at him because even though I was pretty sure I could count on him, I did not want anyone else to know about how much I did to help my mom.

Logan showed up in nine minutes. He hadn't combed his hair, and he looked as if he needed a shower. "What's the rush?" he grumbled, his lower lip curling into a pout.

"Have a chair," Donovan said.

Logan did as he was told, his long legs sprawling. Everyone else immediately sat down, too, as though Donovan had given a general order.

"Now why don't you tell us about your part

in the computer extortion," Donovan said bluntly.

Logan started, stiffened, and grabbed the arms of the chair for support. He glared at Booth.

"What did you tell them?" he demanded.

"Nothing," Booth said. "Not a word. The story came out through . . . uh . . . other means." He glanced at Mom, and Logan turned to stare at her.

"She doesn't know anything about it. She couldn't."

"Porter must have told her," Booth said.

"I knew I couldn't trust him," Logan said, making a fist.

"Logan," I asked, "do you want to hear the whole thing the way Mom will tell it, or do you want to give your own side of the story?"

Logan looked questioningly at Donovan.

Donovan shrugged and added, "It's up to you."

Logan squeezed his eyes shut, ran his fingers through his hair, then over his face. It did nothing to improve his appearance, but it seemed to help pull him together. "I needed money," he started to explain. "The *Teapot* deal fell through. I was desperate. About then I met this guy who's an experienced hacker—into electronics in a big way. He was talking about a HERF gun, and I—"

"A what?" Donovan interrupted his note taking.

"A HERF gun. It's a high energy radio frequency device that sends heavy-duty electronic emissions. You can aim it at a computer site that isn't shielded and wipe out data."

Mom pulled a small notebook and pen from her handbag and began to make notes. This HERF gun stuff may not have been in the novel she just finished, but she could add it to the revision. That's one thing you can count on with writers. They are always searching for ideas, so if something unusual comes up, they take notes.

There was a crinkle of paper behind me. I glanced around and saw Carlos writing down everything, too. I made a mental note to ask him why later.

Donovan asked, "I take it you wiped out some of the Harmony Chocolates Company computer data?"

"Well, yeah," Logan admitted. "I sent an e-mail letter to Porter, telling him to leave one hundred thousand dollars in a manila envelope on his desk, or I'd wipe out more sites."

"Isn't this a family company?" Donovan asked. "Don't you have an interest in improving the company's operations?"

Logan's face twisted. "I don't have a job there, if that's what you're asking. Grandfather doesn't have any use for me. Porter thinks—thought— that I couldn't do anything right. So why should I care about improving the company's operations?"

"Okay, go on," Donovan said. He turned a page in his notebook. "You wanted money. Did you get it?"

Logan shook his head. "I was sloppy. I forgot that the e-mail could be traced to the computer I used. They put things together. I'd been seen at the computer, so it was just a matter of time until they knew I'd sent the message."

Booth broke in. "Porter had a long, serious talk with Logan about the error of his ways. He was really angry about the loss of some of the company's data. However, I pointed out to Porter that there was no point in bringing criminal charges against Logan. After all, Logan *is* family."

"Oh, sure I am," Logan said bitterly.

Mom had been studying Logan. "Was your grandfather told what you had done?"

"No," Logan said.

"You're sure?"

"Porter promised he wouldn't tell him. I think that Porter was afraid that Grandfather would be angry with him, too. Grandfather wasn't happy when Porter computerized the company."

"So you didn't trust Porter," Mom said as she raised one eyebrow. "You were desperately afraid he would tell and you'd be left out of your grandfather's will. You'd go to any lengths to keep that from happening."

Logan's eyes snapped wide open. Alexa gasped. But I tugged at Mom's arm. "Not yet," I whispered so only she could hear me. "You can't accuse him of murder. We don't have all the facts."

"Don't try your tricks on me, Madeline," Logan said. "They won't work. I watch TV, too. Those amateur detectives, like you, get everybody into a room, just like this one, and then they pick one poor slob and tell him why he's the murderer. He falls apart and admits to the crime, then gives all the details, step by step."

He glowered. "Get real, Madeline. This isn't one of your books. This isn't TV. It isn't even virtual reality. This is real life where no one admits anything. The accused hire a bank of good lawyers and go to court swearing they're innocent."

Mom looked shaken. I hated Logan for scolding her publicly, so I turned to Logan and said sternly, "Pay attention, Logan. Mom didn't say *you did anything*. She just pointed out the reason you could have. And maybe you didn't notice, but she did lead you right into blabbing about how you tried to rip off your own relatives. You did a great job of running off at the mouth."

Logan's face turned red, and I was sure that behind me Carlos smothered a chuckle.

Donovan charged in and took over. "During the dinner party last night you met with Porter in this room," he told Logan.

Logan's eyes widened and he shivered. "How'd you know that?"

"You just confirmed it," Donovan said. "So keep going. Why did you need to see Porter? And *what* did you talk about?"

Logan gave a deep sigh and sank back in the chair. "I wanted to make sure that Porter wasn't going to tell Grandfather what I had done with that HERF gun. As Alexa said before, I'd found out that the stock that was in my name wasn't exactly in my name. I mean, it was, but Grandfather had the power to take the stock back, if he wanted to."

"What did Porter say?"

"He said he didn't have time to talk to me. He had a lot to think over."

"Did you see anyone else with Porter while you were there?"

Logan shook his head.

"Can you tell me what time it was when you were in the room?"

Again Logan shook his head. "I ate my salad . . . or at least some of it. I wasn't hungry. I didn't know what Porter was going to do. I had to talk to him."

Alexa spoke up. "Logan arrived soon after I left. I was waiting for the elevator when the doors opened and Logan barged out. He was in such a hurry he didn't even see me."

Her smile looked like the grin on the Cheshire cat as she said to Mom, "You've heard the facts. Yesterday evening Gustave met with Booth and Porter *before* dinner. Then, after the salad course, Booth went to the suite to talk to Porter again. I came next, then Logan. So . . ." Her smile became even broader. "We can prove Porter was alive right up until Logan's visit, which should let everyone off the hook . . . except Logan."

Logan gasped and clutched the arms of his chair. He pleaded with Mom, "Hey, listen, Madeline, I take back everything I said. Maybe it sounded kind of rude. I didn't mean it to be rude. I'm not at my best this early in the morning. I mean—"

"What are you getting at?" Mom asked.

"That we're related. I'm your cousin."

"Three times removed," Mom said. "Or is it five?"

"Whatever. I'm still a cousin. That amateur, mystery-writer detective on TV didn't let her relatives go down the drain when they were accused or arrested. She worked to save them."

"You want me to save you?" Mom asked. "From what?"

"From false arrest," Logan said. "I didn't kill Porter."

Mom softened. She even reached over and patted Logan's shoulder. "No one said you did, darling. And don't worry. We're here to discover the truth."

Alexa snickered. "He asked you to save him, not find out the truth."

Mom dismissed Alexa's snide words with a quick wave of one hand. "Alexa, dear," Mom said, "your detecting is far too elementary. Let's look at your timeline. It's correct, right up to Logan's visit, but then it breaks down. You're forgetting that one of you—the murderer—could easily have paid Porter another visit. There was plenty of time."

I broke in. "I saw Alexa and some of the others leave more than once," I said.

"Of course you did," Alexa said. "I had to powder my nose."

Claudine threw a quick glance at Donovan. "I had a slight headache. I went to the gift shop to buy aspirin."

"Earlier I ran into an old high-school buddy," Logan said. "I called his room."

Gustave turned pink as he said, "I asked the concierge to look up flight schedules to Chicago. I—I felt the need to get away for a—a rest."

Donovan took notes, but he didn't ask any questions. I thought those were pretty sorry excuses for leaving a dinner party in the middle of dinner. I could tell from the expression on Carlos's face that he shared my opinion.

Alexa looked angry enough to say something really mean and nasty to Mom, but there was a knock at the door and a uniformed officer stepped into the room. He handed Donovan an envelope and left. Donovan pulled out the papers and handed them to Booth. "This subpoena gives me the right to examine both wills," he said.

"I would have given them to you right at the start," Booth said, "but Madeline . . ."

"Madeline knew what she was doing," Donovan said. "Going by the book will keep us from having any legal problems if information from the wills has to be used in a murder trial."

Booth gave his briefcase to Donovan. "There's nothing else in the briefcase but the wills. You can return my case when you return the wills."

"Thank you," Donovan said. He turned to Claudine, who had remained silent through most of the conversation. "Your husband should be awake soon. I need to speak with him as soon as possible."

Claudine didn't flinch. She lazily brushed back her blond hair as she said, "Sergeant Donovan, I'm afraid that won't be possible. Arnold began to wake around seven and seemed agitated, so I thought it best to give him more of the medication Dr. Miles left to help him sleep."

Donovan looked like a volcano ready to blow. His face grew red, and I expected to see steam come out of his ears. "I gave orders," he snapped at Claudine.

"I'm terribly sorry," Claudine said coolly, showing that she wasn't sorry at all. "My husband's welfare is much more important to me than your orders."

Mom rested her hand on Donovan's sleeve. "Why don't we just peek in on dear Arnold?" she said. "We're all concerned about him, and we do want him to get the rest he needs."

"That won't be necessary," Claudine said firmly.

"But extremely important," Mom said. "Arnold is my very own dear cousin . . . once removed."

Donovan had collected himself. "Let's go, Mrs. Harmony. I want to see your husband for myself."

Claudine didn't have a choice. She led the way to the suite she shared with Arnold. Mom and Donovan were right behind her. Carlos and I followed.

Adam was back on duty. He nodded pleasantly to all of us and said, "Mr. Harmony is sleeping like a baby."

In a way I was kind of surprised because I suspected . . . well, face it. I had the feeling all along that the wrong person had been murdered. I mean, it was Arnold Harmony who was changing his will, not Porter.

Detective Donovan didn't seem to share my feelings, and neither did Mom, who was enjoying flipping in and out of her Audrey Downing character, so I kept my thoughts to myself.

We went into the bedroom, where the drapes were closed against the light. Donovan looked down at Arnold, who was gently snoring, and said to Claudine, "When he awakes again, you must call me. Do you understand?"

"I'll do what's best," Claudine answered.

Donovan looked at Adam. "It's important that I talk to Mr. Harmony as soon as possible."

Adam nodded, but I hoped Donovan didn't count on Adam making the call. He was being paid by Claudine, so he was more likely to do what *she* told him to do.

Without another word Donovan strode out, and we trailed along behind. I was beginning to feel like the last band in the parade.

"I'm going to headquarters to take a look at the wills," Donovan said.

"I'd like to go with you, Sam," Mom said.

"Sorry, Madeline," Donovan told her. "I've got to put my notes together, write a report, and talk to the lieutenant. By this time he'll have information from the medical examiner's office and the crime lab. I'll see you later."

Mom looked disappointed as he left. "I'm not sure what I should do next," she said.

"Take a break," I told her. "Forget detecting for now. Let's go shopping or walk along the river."

"And have a lovely lunch," Mom said, getting

into the spirit. "I've always enjoyed the restaurant at the Fairmount."

As we walked toward the elevators, Carlos hung back.

"Carlos, we want you to come, too," I said.

"Of course," Mom said, and gave him a big smile.

"Okay! Thanks," Carlos said. "And will you let me take your picture now?" He smiled at me. "I'd like a picture of both of you."

The sunshine was brilliant as we left the hotel and entered the patio. Elsie and Mabel sat at a shaded table sipping from what looked like tall glasses of lemonade. "Yoo hoo," they called, and we smiled at them.

Brilliant red-flowered bougainvillea vines twined around the pillars at each side of the doorway. "Move back," Carlos said. "I want to get the flowers in the shot, too."

Finally he said, "Okay. That looks great. I'll count to three . . ."

The camera clicked, and Carlos said, "Jenny, would you mind taking a picture of me with your mother?"

I traded places with Carlos, but before I could sight the camera, Mom said, "Wait! This sunlight is much too bright. I'm going to run back to the room and get my sunglasses."

What happened next took less than a split second. As Mom turned, a woman screamed, and a man yelled, "Watch out!" I saw what was coming. Without stopping to think, I threw myself at Carlos.

Chapter Eleven

I slammed into Carlos and fell against Mom. She went flying, and I landed on my side, Carlos's elbow in my ribs. I heard a loud thud on the ground next to my head, and dirt flew into my face.

I twisted to see what had happened and came face-to-face with a yellow dwarf hibiscus in what had once been a heavy pottery bowl.

"Jenny! Oh, Jenny, are you hurt?" Mom cried.

Mabel and Elsie rushed up. "That plant just missed her!" Mabel yelled.

"It fell from one of the balconies," Elsie said.

I sat up and looked at Carlos. We were practically nose to nose. His was bleeding.

"You saved my life," he said.

I would have hugged him, but hands were already pulling us to our feet. Elsie had a large, wet cloth napkin and began working on Carlos.

"You're pinching my nose," Carlos complained.

"Be quiet. I have to pinch. That's the only way

to stop the bleeding. Now keep your head back," Elsie ordered.

Mom wrapped her arms tightly around me, nearly smothering me and cutting off my view, but I heard everything Elsie was saying. "Madeline, Mabel and I saw the whole thing. If you hadn't turned away just as the pot fell, it would have hit you."

"And Carlos," I mumbled against Mom's silk blouse, but no one paid attention.

"Janie saved both of you," Elsie said.

"Jenny," I said.

There was a lot more hugging and kissing and Mom's grateful "thank you's," with Elsie, Mabel, Carlos, Mom, and me all squished together. Finally, we broke apart.

"How did the potted plant fall?" Mom asked.

"It just fell," Elsie said. "Down. How else would it fall?"

"I mean, you said you saw everything. So did you see someone accidentally nudge the pot off the balcony? Or push it? Or even throw it?"

"No. We weren't looking up," Mabel said. "We were looking at you."

"Mom!" I shoved back, so I could look into her eyes. "Do you think someone deliberately aimed that heavy pot at you?"

"I don't know," she said.

"Better find out," Mabel said. "You're dragging your feet, Madeline. That mystery-writer sleuth who used to be on television could figure out who committed the crime in less than an hour . . . even including commercials."

I shaded my eyes and looked up at the rows and rows of balconies. "I don't see a single potted plant," I said. "That means it came from inside one of the rooms. Mom, I think we need to visit the hotel's florist and see who might have ordered a potted hibiscus."

"Isn't that just like a teenager," Elsie said. "She has a mother who's an expert at solving crimes, and she tries to tell her what to do."

"Interrogating the hotel florist *was* going to be my next step," Mom told me.

"I guess I'm beginning to know how you think," I said. "Like I know you're also going to find out who sent those fruit and cheese trays."

"Sweetie, you're as clever as Audrey. That's exactly what she would do," Mom said. "Let's go." She raised her chin and headed for the hotel.

I trotted to keep up with her.

"Wait for me!" Carlos called.

This time I didn't mind that Mom was into her Audrey Downing character. Mom would have been scared to death about the potted plant. She would have hung on to me and refused to let me out of her sight. Audrey Downing, on the other hand, was used to walking into danger and getting out of it without a scratch, bruise, or bump. Total fiction. And that's where Mom was now.

But I wasn't. I was scared. Was someone after Mom? Or me? Or both of us? Carlos put an arm around my shoulders, and I smiled at him.

As the three of us entered the chilled fragrance of the hotel's flower shop, I took a long, deep breath and let the mingled perfumes tickle my nose. Mom could do the talking.

The woman in charge of the shop listened to Mom's question, then said, "It's not a matter of ordering potted plants from us. We try to keep a flowering plant in each of the suites as a gift to our special patrons." She smiled. "It's yellow hibiscus this month. Hibiscus goes so well with the Parade of Flowers, don't you think?"

Mom nodded. "That means suites 485 and 487 would each have a potted hibiscus?"

The woman looked a little puzzled, then said, "That's correct. All our suites. Is there anything else I can do for you?"

"Yes, thank you," Mom answered. "Can you tell me which department of the hotel to contact to have cheese and fruit trays sent to the guests' rooms?"

"Oh, this shop takes care of those orders, too. We have a number of lovely baskets in different price ranges," the woman said. She opened a book. "To whom would you like to send a tray?"

"Actually I'd like to find out about yesterday's orders," Mom told her. "How many guests who were here to attend the Harmony party received the trays?"

"Oh, I remember that," the woman answered. "Only two. One to suite 485 and one to suite 487. Mr. Harmony's personal business manager ordered them." She smiled. "We sell Harmony Chocolates in our gift shop. They're really delicious. You might like to try some."

"Thank you for your help," Mom said. As soon as we left the shop, she said, "Next stop, fourth floor. I want to see if a potted plant is missing from either of the Harmony suites."

When we reached the door of 487, Mom knocked lightly. Adam opened the door and smiled when he saw us. "Mr. Harmony's still sleeping," he said.

Mom smiled back. "We didn't come about dear Arnold, although I'm glad to hear that his slumbers are peaceful," she said. "It's about a pot-ted yellow hibiscus the flower shop sent to your suite."

"A potted yellow hibiscus? I don't know what a hibiscus is, but there's a plant with yellow flow-ers in here on the coffee table."

"That's the one. I'm sure of it."

I heard muttered grumbles behind Adam, and Claudine struggled to the door with the heavy pot. "Take it," she grunted. "Keep it. If it's from you, I don't want it!" She thrust it forward, and Carlos grabbed it just in time.

"Oh, but it's not—" Mom began.

"Go away," Claudine said, and slammed the door.

A housekeeping cart stood outside of an open door down the hall. While Carlos struggled to remain upright, Mom called out to the house-keeper, "Hello? Can you help us, please?"

A woman popped into the hallway. "Where are you going with the plant?" she asked suspi-ciously.

"We're trying to return it," Mom said. "We think it belongs in suite 485. Would you mind opening the door for us?"

The housekeeper's eyes narrowed even more. "You're not staying in suite 485."

"No, but the potted hibiscus is."

"How'd it get out?"

Carlos sighed, and his knees began to wobble.

"Sometimes they escape," I said. "They can't be allowed to do that."

"Hmmm," Mom said. "Interesting idea. It's a known fact that plants do get nervous. What if the reactions of a plant were the only clue to the identity of a murder?"

"There was a murder in this room last night," the housekeeper said.

"We know," Mom told her. "We're trying to solve it."

"This plant is getting heavier and heavier," Carlos complained.

"That's worse than nervous," I said to the housekeeper. "Please let us into the suite so Carlos can put the plant down."

The housekeeper wasn't into my kind of humor because she frowned, but she pulled out a passkey and opened the door. She stood where she could watch our every move as Mom, Carlos, and I walked into the living room of the suite.

"No potted plant," I said.

"Can I put it down now? Please!" Carlos gasped.

"Yes. On the coffee table," Mom said.

"Is that all you want?" the housekeeper asked.

"That's it," Mom said. "Thank you for your kind help."

I couldn't resist it. As we left the room, I pointed my finger at the plant. "This time stay put," I told it. "We're not going to chase after you again."

The housekeeper scowled at me as she locked the suite and went back to the room she'd been cleaning.

"We can be fairly sure that the pot that was thrown at us came from Porter's suite," Mom said.

"Alexa, Booth, Logan, and Gustave heard you tell Carlos where and when you'd pose for his picture," I said. "Any one of them could have stayed in the suite and watched for us to show up on the patio. Then it was just aim the plant and boom! How do we find out which one it was?"

"We have to ask the right questions," Mom said.

"I don't get it," I told her. "Why does someone want to kill us?"

"Because we know too much." Mom mysteriously glanced over her shoulder at me and spoke in her Audrey Downing voice.

"Cut it out, Mom," I said, my exasperation beginning to rise again. "We don't know anything."

"We're learning," she said, quoting Audrey. "One by one, we're collecting our snippets of information. We're linking them together. We're studying our suspects. We're reacting to their body language. We're—"

"It doesn't take much body language to throw a potted plant at somebody," I muttered.

Mom looked at her watch. "When people start getting cranky, it means they're hungry. Let's walk down to the Fairmount and have lunch."

Sometimes people turn around and stare at Mom. Sometimes I can see their minds going through the "Who's that?" routine before they realize she's Madeline Jakes, the famous mystery writer. Mom never seems to mind. In fact, I'm sure she enjoys being recognized.

We got the looks and the gasps and one request for an autograph on the way to the Fairmount, but once inside the hotel's light, cool restaurant, everything was quiet and peaceful. People in hotels like the Fairmount don't eat, they dine. And they think it's really uncool to gape.

"This is such a lovely, restful city," Mom said with a happy sigh. "Everything moves at a slower, more peaceful pace." She waved an arm toward the river view and collided with a waiter, who was bringing us tall glasses of iced tea.

"Well, *almost* everything," Mom added. She snatched a fistful of napkins and helped the waiter mop up the puddles on the table.

"Restful?" I echoed and thought hard, grasping the thought that popped into my mind. It suddenly made sense so I said, "No one goes to Chicago for a rest."

Mom and Carlos looked at me as if I'd flipped.

Mom accepted a dry napkin from the waiter. She tucked it on to my lap and said pleasantly, "Of course they don't, sweetie."

"But Gustave said he was going to. Remember? He said he left the dinner party in order to ask the hotel's concierge to look up flight schedules to Chicago. He wanted to get away for a rest."

"Now that is very odd," Mom said.

"Not if he gave the wrong reason," I said. "Last June, when we were in Chicago for the American Booksellers Association convention, some people at your autograph party were talking about a famous candy company based in Chicago. Fanny Farmer. Yes, that's the name. They said that Fanny Farmer Chocolates were the best in the world."

"Just what are you getting at?" Mom asked, but Carlos had already caught up with me.

"Gustave complained that the recipe that made Harmony Chocolates famous really belonged to him," Carlos said. "What if Gustave had plans to sell it to the company in Chicago?"

The waiter arrived to take our orders. We waited until he left before we said anything more.

"Legally, the recipe belongs to Harmony Chocolates," Mom said.

"It's pretty obvious that Gustave doesn't think that being legal also means being right," I reminded her.

Mom thought a moment. "We need to talk to Sam," she said. "Gustave may be our murderer."

"Not yet, Mom," I said. "Just because Gustave *wants* to get his recipe back doesn't mean that he murdered Porter. We have to collect more facts." I sighed and added, "Besides, there's something I don't understand. Since Gustave believes that Arnold Harmony stole his family recipe, why would he murder Porter instead of Arnold?"

"Hmmm. Good point," Mom said. She took a sip of tea.

"Maybe he got the rooms mixed up," Carlos said.

"No way. He'd been to Porter's suite to talk to him," I said.

Mom got out her notebook and began to write.

"Are you putting down what we said about Gustave?" I asked.

She looked up, surprised. "No," she answered, "and I suppose I should. I was making a note to buy some fresh mint when we get home. This iced tea is delicious."

Carlos nudged me. "Don't look over your left shoulder," he said.

"Why not?" I asked and twisted to look.

Alexa and Booth had just come in and were being seated at a table. They were busy frowning at each other, as though they'd had an argument. They didn't see me.

I lowered my voice and said, "Don't look, Mom, but Alexa and Booth just came in. They're over there, by the door."

Mom's head snapped up. She looked, she smiled, she even waved.

113

"Mom, they're suspects," I muttered. "You don't smile and wave at suspects."

"It doesn't hurt to be polite," Mom said. "Audrey Downing is always—"

"You're not Audrey Downing. She's only a make-believe character."

"She's *my* creation," Mom told me. "She comes out of my mind and—"

"That's what I'm trying to tell you," I said. "Audrey's *out* of your mind, but you're *in* your mind. I mean, you're you. You're not Audrey Downing. You're not make-believe. You're a mystery writer. *You are not a real detective.*"

Mom shook her head. "Jenny, my sweet, whatever you're trying to say has become quite confusing."

As the waiter placed our salads in front of us, I shot a quick glance toward Alexa and Booth. To my surprise the table was empty. "They left," I said.

"Who?" Mom asked.

"Alexa and Booth."

Mom paused, a small piece of romaine halfway to her mouth. "Curious," she said.

Carlos poked at the greens on his plate. "Maybe they went out for a burger and fries," he commented.

"Or maybe they didn't want to be in the same room with us," I said. "They know you're trying to find Porter's murderer, Mom."

Mom went back to her salad. "Even suspects have to eat," she said.

I recognized that Audrey Downing line from

one of her books. Frustrated, I gritted my teeth and muttered, "Get real, Mom."

Mom gave me one of those *behave yourself* looks. "As soon as we finish lunch," she said, "I'm going to try to get in touch with Sam. There are some things we have to talk about."

"Like the potted plant," Carlos said, "and what you figured out about Gustave and the Chicago candy connection."

"Exactly," Mom said.

"And Sam Donovan needs to give *you* some information," I reminded her. "Like what was in both those wills."

"The wills. Of course."

For an instant Mom looked surprised, as though she'd forgotten all about the wills. But I hadn't. I felt sure that the information in those wills would lead us directly to Porter Harmony's murderer.

Chapter Twelve

When we got back to our room in the hotel, the message light on the phone was blinking. Mom checked in for the message and smiled broadly as she hung up the receiver.

"Sam called," she said and looked at her watch. "He's meeting Booth Dockman in suite 485 in twenty minutes and wants me to be there."

"And me," I said. "Carlos and I want to go to the meeting, too."

"You're both invited," Mom said. "Not by Sam, but by me. And considering my record of cases solved, that's every bit as official."

Was that Audrey speaking? Or Mom? This time I didn't care. I wanted to get to that meeting.

To our surprise, when we entered the hallway and prepared to knock at the door of suite 485, the housekeeper who had let us in earlier peered out from behind an open door marked LINEN CLOSET and pointed at us. "There they are!

Just like I told you! The plant stealers!" she shouted.

An elderly man, dressed in a suit and tie, stepped into view. "I'm Phil Johnson, with hotel security," he said and held out a folder with an I.D. card in it. "Mrs. Walker was just informing me that you had stolen a plant from suite 485."

"It was not *stolen*," Mom explained. "We put a plant inside 485."

"It was *stolen*!" Mrs. Walker insisted. "First, there's no plant in 485, but there's a plant in 487. Then, they bring a plant to 485, but I take a look in 487, and their plant is gone. Right away I realize that they switched the plants. This is no business of mine. But the missing plant is, because I'll have to account for it. So tell me. What did they do with the missing plant?"

"It was thrown at us," Mom answered calmly.

"Thrown at you?" Mr. Johnson asked in amazement.

Carlos pointed at me. "She wasn't hurt, but I ended up with a bloody nose."

"What?"

Mom continued to explain. "We discovered from the woman who manages the flower shop that pots of yellow hibiscus had been sent to all the hotel suites, including 485 and 487. It seemed possible that the flowerpot had been thrown from one of these balconies, so we inquired first at suite 487."

"Mrs. Harmony in 487 shoved the pot at us," Carlos said, "and we had to put it down someplace, so we put it in 485."

117

"With the help of Mrs. Walker here from housekeeping," Mom added. "We knew no one was in 485 because yesterday evening the occupant had been murdered. We found that the pot of hibiscus that was supposed to be in 485 was missing, so we determined *it* was the pot that had been thrown at us."

Mr. Johnson took a step backward. "You're telling me that the dead man's ghost, or spirit, or whoever you think it was, threw a potted plant at you?"

Mom sighed. "Don't be absurd," she said. "This isn't a horror novel. You've been reading too much Stephen King."

Mr. Johnson frowned and pointed a finger at Carlos. "Wait a minute. I recognize you. You're a bellman at the hotel. Why are you out of uniform?"

"It's my day off," Carlos said. "I'm here helping to solve a crime."

"Call the police," Mrs. Walker loudly whispered to Mr. Johnson. "They're all crazy."

"There's no need to call the police. *I'm* the police." Detective Sam Donovan spoke from behind us, and I wondered how long the door to the suite had been open and he'd been listening. "This is Madeline Jakes, the mystery novelist, and her assistants."

"Do either of you read mysteries?" Mom asked eagerly.

Mrs. Walker shook her head. Mr. Johnson said, "I don't have time to read anything besides the newspaper and *TV Guide*."

"Trust me," Donovan said to Mr. Johnson. "The situation no doubt happened just the way they said it did."

"I—I had a little trouble following just what it was they did," Mr. Johnson answered.

Mrs. Walker scowled at us. "I didn't. It's very simple. They stole a plant from 485. Then they got one from 487 and put it in 485. They're going to have to pay for it. It's not coming out of my salary."

"Of course it isn't, dear," Mom said. "We'll soon find our murderer and everything will be put right."

"Speaking of which," Sam said, "we've got a meeting to keep." He put a hand on Mom's shoulder and escorted her out of the hallway and into the room.

Carlos and I followed, and to my surprise not only Booth Dockman was on hand, but Alexa, Gustave, Logan, and Claudine. They didn't look any happier at seeing us than I was at seeing them. Carlos and I settled next to each other on one of the long sofas.

"I don't know why you insisted that we be here," Gustave complained to Donovan. "I have work to do at the Harmony offices. I can waste no more time here at the hotel."

"It's Sunday, dear," Mom said. "Don't you take weekends off?"

Gustave withdrew, grumbling something under his breath, but Mom didn't let go. In fact, she moved in for the kill. "Why didn't you tell us you'd planned a meeting with the Fanny

Farmer Chocolate Company in Chicago?" she asked.

Gustave gasped, then stammered, "H-How d-did you know?"

"Elementary," Mom said. Was she Audrey now or Sherlock Holmes? Or Audrey playing Sherlock Holmes? Mom was enjoying her role. "Did you actually think that the people at Fanny Farmer would buy a stolen recipe from you?"

Gustave's face went from white to red. "That recipe was stolen from *me*!"

Mom took a pair of glasses from her purse, stared at Gustave through them for a full minute, then pushed them up on her head. They made her look a lot like the mystery-writer detective on TV. "Detective Donovan," she said, "you may have your murderer right here."

I tugged at Mom's sleeve and whispered in her ear, "Not yet, Mom. You only have guesses, not real facts."

"On the other hand . . . ," Mom said sweetly, and sat down on the sofa, next to me.

"The fruit and cheese trays," I prompted.

"On the other hand," Mom repeated, "we've been ignoring Alexa and her little expenditures."

Alexa, who'd been lounging back against the large cushions in her chair, sat bolt upright. For the first time I saw alarm in her eyes. "Just what do you mean by that?" she asked.

"Dear Alexa, there's no need to pretend," Mom said. Encouraged by Alexa's reaction, Mom slid completely into Audrey Downing's character and dramatic dialogue. "You left an easy paper trail," Mom added.

Paper trail? A signature for two fruit and cheese trays? Mom was over the edge on this one.

But Alexa jumped to her feet. She began to pace, and her mouth turned on like a water faucet. "Okay, okay. So you found out about *Happiness Unlimited.* I can easily explain those checks. It was a matter of my bookkeeping system. Normally I'd have a certain amount of expenses listed under *miscellaneous.* Right? Well, I hate dull, meaningless words like that, so I simply labeled the miscellaneous expenses *Happiness Unlimited,* and my whole day grew brighter."

"How much money are we talking about?" Claudine's eyes narrowed.

"Around twenty thousand," Alexa said quickly.

Claudine gasped and asked, "How could you possibly have miscellaneous expenses of twenty thousand dollars? What did the expenses cover?"

"Me," Alexa said. "They covered *me.* As Arnold Harmony's personal business manager, I had to attend all those lovely fund-raisers and social events with the cream of society. Naturally that demanded beautiful clothing for each event. I couldn't appear in the same old things all the time, could I?"

"Did Arnold Harmony know about these clothing expenditures?" Donovan asked.

"Yes, and he had no objections."

The corners of Claudine's mouth turned down and she muttered, "I'm sure he hadn't."

"How about Porter Harmony?" Mom asked. "Did he know?"

"Yes!" Alexa practically spat the word at Mom.

Mom didn't seem to mind. "Did you tell him?"

"No," Alexa said. "Someone in Neiman's credit department . . . well, that's neither here nor there, is it?"

Mom didn't have a chance to answer. Donovan asked Alexa, "Were these expenditures the basis of your discussion with Porter Harmony last night?"

"No," Alexa said. She looked him right in the eye as she spoke, but I had the funny feeling she wasn't telling the truth. Or maybe that she was telling part of the truth that answered his question, but was holding something back.

I had to remind myself that I'd had the same feeling about Logan—even before we'd found out what he'd done with the HERF gun—and Gustave, before I made the connection to the Fanny Farmer Chocolate Company. Maybe I was just too suspicious about each and every one of these suspects. I reminded myself of what Uncle Bill had once told me: "A good detective keeps her mind open and doesn't jump to quick conclusions."

Donovan fixed an eagle eye on Alexa. She squirmed a little, but she stared right back. "In Arnold Harmony's previous will—the one which would be legally binding until the new will is signed—you were appointed to the well-paid and

122

well-funded position of managing the Arnold Harmony Memorial Charity Foundation," he said.

"That's right," she told him.

"Was that part of the will changed?" Mom interrupted. "Did Cousin Arnold cut Alexa out?"

"I don't know," Alexa said. "I don't know what's in the new will."

"Then you tell us, please, Sam," Mom said.

"I don't know either," Donovan said.

"But Sam, you have both wills. You have to know," Mom insisted.

Donovan shook his head. "No, I don't," he said, and he stared at Booth as he spoke. "There was only one envelope in the briefcase you gave me, and it contained a single copy of what must have been Arnold Harmony's first will, judging by the date."

Booth's mouth opened so wide he looked like a puppet. I expected someone to pull a string to make him talk. He sputtered a bit before he managed to say, "I don't understand it. What happened to the new will? It was in a second envelope."

Everyone stared at Booth. I looked at each face, trying to see if any of them were putting on an innocent act. I didn't think they were. They all looked astonished. Someone in this room was putting on a good act. Who?

"I hoped you could tell me what happened to the new will," Donovan said to Booth.

"I don't know. Someone must have taken it out of my briefcase," Booth answered.

"During last evening and again today, was your briefcase ever left unattended?"

"W-Why, yes." Booth looked miserable. "I—I saw no harm. I didn't anticipate a . . . a thief."

"I'm sure Booth created more than one copy of the will," Mom said. "You did, didn't you, dear?"

"Yes, of course," Booth said, but he looked even more glum. "Three copies, to be exact. But the copies were all together in that envelope, ready to be signed. The thief got all of them."

"Oh, dear," Mom said.

"Does your secretary use a computer?" I asked.

"Why, yes," Booth said.

"Then is it possible that the will is still in the computer?"

"I honestly don't know," he said. "I could call Marcie—she's my secretary—and ask her to go to the office and see if the will's still in the computer. If it is, she can run off a copy and bring it to the hotel."

"Fine," Donovan said and motioned toward the phone. "Call her now, please."

Booth dialed the phone, and his expression changed from hope to despair. He relayed Donovan's instructions and hung up. "She's out," he said. "I only got her answering machine."

"You and I can take a little trip to your office," Donovan said.

Booth looked even more miserable. "It won't do any good. I never quite got the hang of using a computer. I leave all that up to Marcie."

"No problem. I can do it," Donovan said, "but

before we leave I have a few things to discuss with everyone here."

I pulled Mom down to the sofa, while the others—looking shocked and scandalized—all began to talk at the same time.

"Mom," I whispered, "only Booth knows everything that was in those wills. Just in case the will's already been deleted from the computer, try to find out how much he remembers by asking him now."

Mom sat up and clapped her hands. Startled, everyone stopped talking and looked at her. "Thank you for your attention," she said. "Now, Booth, as a professional, as a lawyer, I'm sure you can remember what Arnold asked you to put into the new will. So why don't you think hard and answer my earlier question?"

Booth stared vacantly. "What was the question?"

Mom smiled graciously and then quickly looked at me. "What was the question? Even Jenny remembers, dear."

"Of course, Mom," I said wearily. "In the new will did Alexa still have the same job managing the Arnold Harmony Memorial Charity Foundation?"

"Yes, that's it exactly," Mom said and repeated the question.

Booth began nodding while she was still speaking. "That part of the will wasn't changed," he said.

Alexa smiled smugly.

"How much of the new will can you remember?" Donovan asked Booth.

"I'm not sure," Booth said. "I'll try my best, but I honestly don't know how much I can bring back."

"Detective Donovan," I blurted out. "Why don't you just ask Arnold Harmony?"

Claudine jumped. "He's still sleeping," she said. "You can't bother him."

Donovan didn't seem surprised, or even upset. "No one's going to bother him," he said. "I've ordered a police guard on his bedroom. The officer will contact me as soon as Mr. Harmony wakes up."

"I'll call Dr. Miles," Claudine challenged as she got to her feet. "He won't let you do this."

"Dr. Miles can see his patient any time he likes," Donovan said firmly. "And you can be with your husband as soon as you answer a few questions. Please be seated."

As Claudine sat down again, Donovan asked Booth, "In Mr. Harmony's previous will, Mrs. Harmony was given an extremely large settlement and all her husband's shares in Harmony Chocolates. Was any of this changed in the new will?"

Booth fidgeted and his cheeks turned pink. "Ummm, it may be breaking a confidence for me to say."

"The will was to be made public last night."

"But, due to circumstances, it wasn't." Booth's lip curled stubbornly.

Claudine sighed. "What difference does it

make? Porter's the one who was killed, not Arnold. If you want to know what I'm supposed to inherit some day, I'll tell you, Detective Donovan. Arnold arranged to give me what you'd probably call 'a comfortable settlement.' "

"I thought Mr. Dockman was the only one who knew the contents of Mr. Harmony's will."

Claudine shrugged. "Yesterday Arnold decided to tell me what my share would be. He said he wanted to . . . to prepare me."

"So you wouldn't make a scene?" Alexa's smile was mean.

"I don't make scenes," Claudine said. "I have other ways of handling problems."

Like murder? I shivered and moved closer to Carlos before I reminded myself that Arnold hadn't been the murder victim.

"It must have been upsetting to you," Donovan said.

"A little at first, I suppose," Claudine answered. "I knew that Arnold was upset about the sapphire jewelry I recently purchased. He said a lot of things I was sure he didn't really mean about how I'd bought too many expensive things for myself. The sapphires were the last straw. I'm telling you this myself, because I'm sure that eventually Arnold will tell you. Anyhow, it was a shock when he told me he had taken away the company stock he was once going to leave to me. I realized that even so, I'd still have a good income, the Rolls Royce, our home in San Antonio, and our vacation villa in the Virgin Islands. Arnold plans to give my share of the company

127

stock to his favorite charities." She shrugged. "I don't care."

"That's very noble of you, darling." Mom beamed at Claudine.

"Grandfather never heard the saying 'Charity begins at home,' " Logan said snidely.

Donovan looked sharply at Logan. "Do you know what plans your grandfather has for you? Did he tell you?"

Logan's eyes were almost slits as he glanced upward, and the corners of his mouth turned down sullenly. "No, but Porter did. He said that Grandfather had shown him a copy of the new will."

"I take it that you came out much better in the old will than in the new one?"

"Arnold didn't like the fact that Logan was always coming around asking for money," Claudine said. "He'd ask his father for what he called a loan. Often Porter turned him down, so he'd ask Arnold. If one of them did give in and lend him money, Logan never paid him back."

"It wasn't like that," Logan butted in. "Claudine's making things up about me."

"Are you saying it isn't true that you asked your father and grandfather for loans?" Donovan asked.

"Oh, I suppose it's true in a way," Logan admitted. "It's just that we may have called them *loans*, but I always felt they were more like loving gifts from devoted relatives."

"Spare us your sentimental false drivel, Logan," Claudine said haughtily. "You're supposed to be telling the truth."

Logan sighed. "You don't know how frustrating it was for me to *never* be able to please Porter *or* Arnold. I asked them both to give . . . uh . . . lend me enough money to support me while I wrote my book, and would they? No."

Logan had said a magic word. "A book?" Mom asked. "What kind of book?"

"It's the story of our family," Logan explained. "My therapist suggested it. 'Your joy, your pain, your experiences with your family members—get it all out on paper,' he said, so that's what I started to do. I'm going to expose all the family secrets, problems, even scandals—legal and illegal—the truth behind the scenes at Harmony Chocolates."

Everyone stared at him silently. Logan might as well have painted a target on the back of his shirt and handed out bows and arrows. Didn't Logan realize that admitting that he knew family and business secrets and was ready to write about them made him an accident just waiting to happen, as far as the murderer was concerned? It gave me a weird feeling to know that Porter Harmony's murderer was probably right here in this room, at this very minute deciding Logan's future.

Mom finally broke the silence. "Logan, you might be *safer* writing about some other topic."

"I read this article about how to write. It said that writers are supposed to write about something they know . . . and that's what I know," Logan replied almost defiantly.

"Perhaps your therapist . . . ," Mom began, but Logan interrupted her.

"Oh, he doesn't know it, but he's going to be in the book, too." Logan added, "If the book ever gets written, that is. Porter informed me that I was cut out of the new will. If I have no funds, how am I supposed to learn to stand on my own two feet?" Logan stared glumly down at his shoes.

Donovan looked at his watch, then said, "Let's move on. Mr. Dockman, you receive a retainer from the Harmony Chocolates Company, do you not?"

"Yes, I do," Booth Dockman answered.

"Was there any provision for you as far as a retainer, settlement, or any substantial amount of money in Arnold Harmony's new will?"

"Absolutely not," Booth said. "An attorney is paid only for services rendered and does not expect to be mentioned in a client's will. I've received what I consider to be a fair retainer from Mr. Arnold Harmony ever since I took my father's place as his attorney."

"So when you met with Mr. Harmony to try to urge him to drop his plans for a public disclosure and signing of the new will, you had no personal interest to protect?"

"None whatsoever," Booth answered.

"And when you spoke privately last night to Porter Harmony, did your inclusion in the will come up?"

"Of course not." Booth puffed up and looked

as though he'd been insulted. He got to his feet and picked up the phone. "I'm going to try Marcie again," he said. He dialed, and this time he was successful, since he talked to someone. As he hung up the phone he sagged with relief. "Marcie said that she deleted the will from the computer, but she filed a temporary copy to keep until a signed copy can be filed," Booth reported. "She's going to get it from my office and bring it here as soon as possible."

"Fine. In that case—" Donovan began, but he was interrupted as the door burst open, and a uniformed policewoman strode through.

"Mr. Harmony's awake, Sergeant," the officer said.

"Good," Donovan said. He closed his notebook with a snap and jammed it into his inner coat pocket.

The officer hesitated. "Except . . . ," she said.

"Except what?" Donovan asked.

"His nurse said it's probably the effect of the medication he was given to sedate him, because he's awake, as I told you. It's just that, well, he's . . ."

"Get to it, officer," Donovan snapped.

The officer blinked and stood at attention. "He's awake, sir," she said, "but he's got a kind of amnesia. He doesn't know who is he or what he's doing in this hotel."

Chapter Thirteen

"Mrs. Harmony, will you please accompany us?" Donovan asked, but Claudine was way ahead of him, marching out the door with a worried look on her face.

We formed a parade again, Carlos and I bringing up the rear, as we strode into suite 487 and stood at the foot of Arnold Harmony's bed.

I smiled at Adam, and he smiled back, but the eyes of everyone else in the room were on Arnold.

He peered out from under the covers, which he held tightly across the lower half of his face. His voice wobbled, and some of his words slurred, but there was no mistaking his irritation. "This is a bedroom," he said, "and you can clearly see that I'm in bed. Who invited all of you to come in here?"

"Oh, darling," Claudine crooned.

Arnold squinted at her. "Do I know you?" he asked.

As Claudine gulped down a little sob and

stepped back, Donovan took charge. "Mr. Harmony," he began.

"Who's Mr. Harmony?" Arnold asked.

"You are," Donovan said. "Your name is Arnold Harmony."

Arnold lifted one bony finger and pointed at Claudine. "Who's the young woman who called me *darling?*"

"Your wife."

Arnold thought a moment. Then he said, "This is very confusing. Everybody get out of here. I think I'll go back to sleep."

Donovan spoke up. "Mr. Harmony, my name is Sam Donovan. I'm a detective with the San Antonio Police Department. I'd like to ask you a few questions."

"I'd like to ask a few questions myself," Arnold said. "For instance, what am I doing here?"

Donovan turned to Claudine. "I think you should call Dr. Miles." He stared at her from under his eyebrows. "But no more sedation."

Mom stepped closer to the bed. "Mental association might help dear Arnold return to reality," she said, and in a clear, soaring soprano, she sang the Harmony Chocolates commercial, ending with "a song in every bite."

When Mom finished, Arnold made a rude noise. "I hate that song," he said. "It ought to be banned from TV."

Mom's feelings weren't hurt. In fact, she smiled. "Well," she said happily, "at least that's a step in the right direction."

Arnold suddenly closed his eyes and began to

snore. "Call his doctor," Donovan told Claudine. He handed her his business card. "And get in touch with me immediately when you find that Arnold is able to remember what he did last night and talk about it."

Claudine shrugged. "I can tell you that. Arnold ate a very light meal, then he lay down for a nap."

"I'd like to hear from Arnold himself."

Glaring defensively, Claudine snapped, "You want to know if he talked privately with Porter? Well, he didn't. I can tell you that. I've been with Arnold night and day. I know everything he's thought, said, and done."

Donovan just repeated, "Please get in touch with me when Arnold is able to talk about last night."

Claudine's eyes narrowed with anger. "I think you've been here long enough," she said. As she led the way out of the bedroom, Donovan, Mom, and Carlos automatically followed her, but I hung back.

"Adam," I said, "do you know if Mr. Harmony had a chance to talk to Porter last night?"

He glanced in the direction Claudine had taken and looked a little nervous. "He was supposed to," Adam said. "Mr. Harmony had arranged for a time when Mrs. Harmony would be hosting the dinner party. He asked me to leave for a little while because their conversation would be private."

As he paused, again glancing toward the door, I asked, "So? What happened?"

"I don't know," he said. "I went down to the lobby and bought a magazine and a candy bar. I strolled around, killing time, then came back. Mr. Harmony was asleep in his chair, and there was no sign that Mr. Porter had come to the suite."

"What kind of sign are you talking about?"

"I'd put out two wine glasses and an ice bucket with a small bottle of white wine in it and a plate of cookies. The wine and cookies were untouched. So I knocked at the door of Mr. Porter's suite to ask when he planned to visit Mr. Arnold. Mr. Porter's door was ajar, so I opened it and went in. That's when I discovered that Mr. Porter had been murdered. You know the rest."

Claudine suddenly appeared in the doorway, elbows wide and her fists resting on her hip bones. "You don't belong here, Jessie," she said to me. "Get out! Right now!"

I broke into a run, passing the policewoman on duty and catching up with my mother and Donovan just as the elevator doors opened. We stepped into an empty elevator, and I said, "Mom, I was able to talk to Adam alone—just as you hoped." Mom looked a little puzzled, then listened intently while I repeated what Adam had told me.

Donovan said, "That's essentially what Adam reported to me, but without the details. I wasn't informed that Arnold was meeting Porter without Claudine's knowledge." He smiled at Mom. "You have good hunches, Madeline."

135

"It's a special intuition," Mom said, beaming at him.

Carlos winked at me, then tucked a small notebook back into his pocket.

As the elevator doors opened and we stepped into the hotel lobby, I asked him, "Mom and Detective Donovan are taking notes because they're trying to solve the crime, but you're taking notes, too. Why?"

"So I won't forget this memorable experience," Carlos said. He smiled so beguilingly that I was tempted to drop it, but there was something I absolutely had to know.

"Does your note taking have anything at all to do with the newspaper columnist you give tips to?"

A wounded expression crossed Carlos's face. "Don't you trust me, Jenny?" he asked.

"You promised you wouldn't tell him anything about Mom's sleuthing act."

"I haven't, and I won't." Carlos put a hand over his heart. "I told him your mother was a guest at the hotel, and he said that was old news and didn't even give me my five-dollar fee, because the front page of the paper was full of Porter Harmony's murder and the reporter made a big thing out of your mother being one of the guests invited to Arnold Harmony's party."

"I'm sorry," I said. "I feel like I'm Mom's protector or something, especially now, when she's partly my mother and partly her Audrey Downing character. I don't want anyone to hurt her. Do you know what I mean?"

"How's Audrey Downing at solving mysteries?"

"Fine, since Mom's made them up and knows from the start who the murderer is. But Audrey's as limited as Mom is with the real thing."

Carlos smiled. "From what I've seen so far, Jenny Jakes is pretty good at picking out important information and uncovering important facts."

"To a point," I said. "What I've learned from Uncle Bill and from reading lots of mysteries helps, but I don't know if I can solve this mystery, because I've never tried solving one."

"Hey, don't worry. I'm here to help," Carlos said.

We both laughed, although I realized that so far Carlos had just watched and listened and hadn't discovered a single clue to help us figure out who killed Porter Harmony.

While Carlos and I had been talking, Mom and Donovan had walked off in the direction of the coffee shop. I could see them standing in line, an awfully happy smile on my mother's face, and for an instant I wondered what she was getting into. Did she have to be watched every minute?

Donovan's phone beeped, and he answered it. With a startled look he snapped the phone shut and strode back toward the elevators. Mom trotted to keep up.

While Donovan jabbed at the elevator buttons, Mom grabbed my hand. "Jenny!" she cried. "Sam was just contacted by Booth Dockman. All Booth said was, 'Come quickly. Mr. Harmony is dead!' "

Chapter Fourteen

When we reached suite 487, Donovan pounded on the door. To my surprise Adam opened the door and spoke in a low whisper. "Mr. Arnold is still sleeping," he said.

We stared at him. Donovan finally found his voice and said, "Sleeping? I was told that Mr. Harmony had died."

Adam looked surprised. "It must have been a prank call," he said. "You can come in and see Mr. Arnold, if you don't believe me. He's snoring peacefully."

"Who'd play a terrible trick like that?" Mom asked.

Donovan looked just as puzzled but said emphatically, "There's no question who made the call. It was Booth Dockman."

"Why would Booth—" Mom began.

"There's a third Mr. Harmony," I interrupted. "Logan Harmony."

Mom gasped. "Oh, dear. Do you suppose Booth meant Logan?"

The door to suite 485 opened and Booth poked his head around it. "I thought I heard you out here," he said. "Why haven't you come in?"

"You told me that Mr. Harmony was dead," Donovan said. "I assumed that you meant Mr. Arnold Harmony."

"I was upset," Booth said. "I suppose I didn't make myself clear. It's Logan."

We filed into the living room of suite 485. Mom, Carlos, and I stopped near the doorway, but Donovan walked over to Logan, who was lying facedown on the floor. Donovan knelt next to him. There was a weird foul smell in the room. I was thankful I couldn't see Logan's face.

Claudine, Alexa, Gustave, and Booth stood by the window, as far away from the body as they could get.

"Booth told us we must remain in the room until you arrived," Gustave said, "so we did. Now may we leave?"

"No," Donovan answered.

Mom glanced at the table, which was filled with dirty dishes. "You ate lunch here?" she asked in surprise. "At the scene of Porter's murder?"

"We were hungry," Alexa said.

"But the coffee shop—?"

"We wanted privacy," Claudine said.

I whispered to Mom, "If they ordered from room service, the meal charges would be billed to this room."

Donovan sniffed at something he held in his

hand. "Cyanide," he said. "Not only can I recognize the flush on Logan's face, I can smell the poison." He held out what looked like a piece of a fortune cookie to Mom. "Do you agree, Madeline?"

"Yes. Bitter almonds," Mom-Audrey said. "Unfortunately I've seen its effect before."

"Aw, c'mon, Mom," I whispered. "You have not."

As Donovan got to his feet, he asked, "How many of you ordered Chinese food?"

"Only Logan," Booth answered. "You can count on Logan ordering Chinese food if it's on the menu. He loves it."

"He's the only one who received a fortune cookie?"

"That's correct."

Donovan turned to Mom. "It looks as though he died clutching part of the cookie. As you know, cyanide works very quickly."

"Yes," Mom said. She sighed. "I wonder what the poor boy's fortune was."

"Don't touch it," Donovan said. "Don't touch anything. We have to keep the scene intact until the crime lab gets here." He looked at the group by the window. "Which one of you wants to give me the details about what happened?"

Booth shook his head. "We don't know what happened. We ordered from room service, and a waiter rolled in this table with the food on it. Nothing went wrong until Logan finished his lunch and began to eat his fortune cookie."

"I'll want to talk to your waiter," Donovan said.

"That's something *I* can help with," Carlos told him. "I'll check with room service, find out who their waiter was, and bring him up here." Donovan nodded, and Carlos shot out of the room.

Donovan dialed his cellular phone, spoke briefly, and told us, "The crime lab and medical examiner are on their way."

The door slammed open. Carlos entered with a scared-looking guy his own age following closely behind.

"This is Pete Stevens," Carlos said. "He brought the lunch order to the suite."

Pete's eyes bugged out as he stared at Logan's body. The color drained out of his face. He leaned against the wall and stammered, "I—I didn't do it."

"Nobody said you did. Detective Donovan just wants to ask you some questions."

Carlos gave Pete an encouraging slap on the back as Donovan asked, "Mr. Stevens, did you deliver the lunch order to this room?"

"Y-Yes," Pete answered.

"Was one of the orders for a plate of Chinese food?"

"The Oriental Stir-Fry," Pete said.

"Which comes with a fortune cookie for dessert?"

"No, sir," Pete said. "No fortune cookie."

"You did not deliver a fortune cookie?"

"No way."

"When you delivered the food, did any of the guests approach the table before the others?"

Pete gave a quick glance to everyone in the room. He nodded toward Mom and me. "Those two weren't here," he said.

"How about the others?"

Pete's color began to come back. I think he even blushed. "Well . . . uh . . . as soon as I rolled the table into place, they all rushed up and crowded around. I had to ask them to move back so I could raise the sides of the table and set up the places."

"Did any of them touch the food?"

He nodded, and his face grew redder. "The lady with the red hair said, 'I'm starving!' and began lifting the covers from the plates to see what was under them. Then the lady with the blond hair poked her finger in the whipped cream on a piece of chocolate pie." He pointed at Gustave. "That gentleman grabbed the pie and said, 'Keep your hands out of my pie. I have no intention of sharing it.' The man lying on the floor over there kept saying, 'If you see a fortune cookie, it's mine.'" Pete gulped and added, "They were like all over the food. I asked for someone to sign for the order. Mr. Dockman signed, and I got out of here fast."

"Is there anything else you can remember about the delivery?" Donovan asked.

Pete thought a minute. "I don't think so," he said.

Donovan gave him his card. "If you think of anything I should know, please get in touch with me."

As Pete left, Alexa said, "Look, we were hungry. It wasn't as gross as that kid said it was."

"I *accidentally* stuck my finger in Gustave's pie," Claudine said.

"Which made the pie less appetizing," Gustave grumbled.

Booth frowned at Donovan. "I don't know why you're questioning us," he said. "We had nothing to do with the preparation or delivery of the food."

"Now, Booth," Mom chided. "You heard what Pete Stevens told us. The food order did not include the poisoned fortune cookie. That means it had to have been put on the table by someone else in the room."

Booth, Alexa, Claudine, and Gustave were silent as they studied each other.

As Mom went on, I recognized her switch into Audrey Downing. "Booth, it's time to face facts," Mom said. "You know what I mean . . . about taking stock."

Booth stiffened. "Taking stock? What are you telling me?"

Mom smiled that enigmatic smile, which told me that once again she had drifted off into Audrey and had no idea what she or anyone else was talking about. However, the smile didn't affect Booth that way. He dropped into the nearest chair toward the window.

"It was a temporary loan," he said, his mouth

144

twisting with bitterness. "Go on. Tell the detective the rest of it. Somehow you found out, Madeline, and now that you've told, the harm's been done." He put his head into his hands.

Mom, blinking with amazement, just stood there. I stepped in, since Booth's reaction to *taking stock* made perfect sense to me. "Selling company stock without authority is a major offense, isn't it?" I asked. "Don't count on my Mom to smooth the way for you. You'll have to tell Detective Donovan about your activities yourself."

"Really, there isn't much to tell," Booth said from behind his fingers. "I have Arnold's power of attorney. Some personal investments of mine had failed. I was in deep financial trouble. I used some of Arnold's stock in Harmony Chocolates as collateral for a loan. As I said, it's temporary. I intend to rectify the matter as soon as possible. No one knew about it until now. No one."

The medical examiner and the people with the crime lab arrived, and we were all asked to leave. Donovan instructed Alexa, Booth, Gustave, and Claudine to stay in the hotel, where they could be reached for questioning.

Mom decided to stick with Donovan, but I had to get out of that room. I pulled Carlos out into the hall and waited until I was sure we couldn't be overheard. "Let's go down to the lobby and wait for that secretary named Marcie."

Carlos looked surprised. "Why wait for her?"

"The person who stole the envelope with the new will in it must have been desperate," I said.

145

"It had to have been taken while the room was filled with party guests. Any one of them could have seen the theft. That was a big chance to take."

"I still don't get why we have to wait for Marcie," Carlos said.

"If the thief is so scared about anyone seeing the will that he'd take one big risk, he's likely to take another one."

"You mean steal the will from Marcie? Right in plain view?"

"It could happen," I said.

"Do you know what Marcie looks like?"

"No," I said, "but she'll be carrying a large manila envelope, and she'll go to the front desk and ask for Booth Dockman. If you want to come with me, let's go."

"Okay. I'm with you," Carlos said.

We took the elevator down to the lobby, where the crowd, who had come for the Fiesta, seemed to have grown even larger. A lot of women were wearing soft white blouses, long ribbon-trimmed skirts, and flowers tucked in their hair. And some of the men wore sombreros. But at the far end of the lobby I spotted a large, lumpy someone in what looked like shapeless, long white skirts covered by a huge black lace mantilla, large enough to wrap around her like a cloak. What I could see of her face under the mantilla was masked.

"Someone is really into dress-up," I told Carlos and nodded toward the strange figure.

146

Carlos, who'd been looking toward the door, turned to see what I was staring at. "Which one?" he asked.

"The woman in the black mantilla over there," I said, and dodged a bellman's cart piled with suitcases.

"Over where?"

I looked again, but there was no sign of the party goer in the weird outfit anymore. "Never mind," I said. "She's gone."

"What was she doing?"

"Nothing. Just looking weird."

"Some people are good at that," Carlos said, and we both laughed.

For the next few minutes we kept our eyes on the door, watching the people entering the hotel. Finally, we spotted a pretty blond woman in a snug flowered-print dress, who impatiently pushed the glass revolving door and darted through the people in the lobby until she reached the front desk. In her hands was a manila envelope. I could just make out Booth Dockman's name on it.

As she slapped the envelope on the front desk, Carlos and I stepped to her side. "Hi, Marcie," I said politely. "Is that envelope for Mr. Dockman?"

"Why are you asking?" she said. "Who are you?"

We didn't have time to answer. The masked person in the mantilla suddenly rose up, shoved Marcie toward us, and reached for the envelope.

147

But I was faster. I snatched the envelope, jumped over a suitcase, and ducked through a line of people waiting to check out.

"Run!" Carlos called to me. "I'll block."

I ran, but I heard Carlos give a loud *"Oooof!"* I didn't dare look back to see if he'd been able to stop the person in the mantilla.

There were people waiting for the elevators, so I ran past them and entered the door marked STAIRS. I didn't want to be trapped in an elevator with that awful person after me.

I made so much noise clattering up the stairs, I couldn't tell if anyone was following me. I opened the door leading to the fourth floor, but stopped as I saw the mantilla person step off the elevator. Unfortunately she—or he—got a good look at me.

I ducked back into the stairway and took the steps two at a time. I began to pant and wheeze and struggled to keep going. *You're in terrible shape*, I told myself. *Go out for track. Run three miles every morning before school. Exercise! You haven't got enough energy to make it to the eighth floor.*

As I paused, trying to catch my breath before I opened the door to the hallway, I saw a small number nine. Nine? I'd run an extra flight?

I turned, ready to go down to *eight,* when I heard a sharp creak just below me. I stopped and slowly, carefully, peeked over the handrail. There, looking up at me, was the masked person in the mantilla.

Chapter Fifteen

My wind and energy back, I raced up to the tenth floor and burst through the door. It didn't take long to spot the room Elsie and Mabel were in. I pounded at the door.

But no one came. Everything was silent.

I groaned with frustration, then pounded again, still hopeful.

The door to the stairs opened, and the mantilla appeared. Slowly, it moved toward me. "Give me the envelope," it whispered.

"No," I said.

"You don't have a choice," it whispered.

Elsie's door opened so suddenly I lost my balance and nearly fell in.

"Janie! It's you?" she said. "Mabel and I were napping when someone began a terrible pounding on our door. Anyone who'd behave like that . . . well, right away Mabel and I knew they were up to no good, so Mabel called security, and they're sending a guard up here right now."

The masked figure took a couple of steps

toward us. I tried to budge Elsie out of the way, but she was as strong as I was and leaned out of the doorway, squinting to take a good look.

"Who in the world is that?" she asked. "Your little friend Carleton? What's the idea of the goofy outfit?"

Near us the elevator bell dinged. The figure jumped, nearly tangling itself in the long skirts and mantilla as it dashed for the door to the stairs. It disappeared just as Mr. Johnson stepped into the hallway.

"You called security?" he asked.

"Sorry about that," Elsie said. "We don't need you. It was only Janie."

But I said, "Someone in this hotel is trying to steal this envelope from me. I have to take it to Detective Donovan. Will you please escort me to suite 485?"

Mr. Johnson did so, grudgingly, because—as he said—he was sure I had no business being there.

Carlos was nervously walking up and down in the hallway outside of suite 485. I was so glad to see him I reached out and hugged him. "The masked person in the black mantilla almost got me," I said.

"I stopped it for a few minutes, but it jabbed me in the stomach and got away." Carlos sounded apologetic.

"I'm not even going to ask for details," Mr. Johnson said.

We knocked at the door, under Mr. Johnson's watchful eye. I asked the officer who answered the door, "Will you please tell Detective Donovan that Jenny Jakes is here and I have Arnold Harmony's will?"

The officer gave a quick nod and rushed to get Sam Donovan.

In less than a minute Donovan and Mom stood in the doorway. I handed the envelope to Donovan. "Someone in a mask and a huge black mantilla tried to take this, but I hung on to it."

"Was this person in costume male or female?" Donovan asked.

"I couldn't tell. There was just a big swirl of white material, like a big, bulky skirt, with the mantilla over it."

"Voice?"

"I don't know. It whispered."

"How about hands?"

"I didn't notice."

"Shoes?"

"I couldn't see the shoes. The skirt—or whatever it was—covered the shoes."

"Describe the costume," Donovan said.

I did, and he sent one of the officers in the room to search the hotel for the person. Then he asked the hotel's security guard to escort Mom, Carlos, and me to our room on the eighth floor.

"I'll join you within half an hour," he said.

I was glad for some quiet time to go over all that had happened.

Once in the room, Mom and I settled into the pair of upholstered chairs, and Carlos sat in the small chair at the desk.

"Jenny, my sweet, you're all right?"

I nodded.

"Then take notes," Mom said, so Carlos and I switched places, and I pulled a pen and some hotel stationery out of the desk drawer.

Mom's forehead wrinkled as she thought. "I do wish we knew what the message was in the fortune cookie," she said. "I can't help thinking that it might be a clue to the identity of the murderer."

"I doubt it, Mom," I said, but she wasn't listening.

"That would be a great clue," she said. "There could be a string of murders, a fortune cookie left with each body. They'd seem like simple innocuous messages, but Audrey could see a pattern and tie them together. Maybe the lottery numbers on the back could be a code and—"

"Mom," I said, trying not to sound as impatient as I felt, "I've told you many times. This is not one of your Audrey Downing mystery novels. We're trying to solve real murders here."

"I know, sweetie," Mom said, but she pulled her own little notebook and pen from her purse. "Just wait a moment while I make some notes to myself. I don't want to lose this thought."

While Mom wrote, I grimaced in Carlos's direction, but he didn't see me. He was busy making some notes in his own small notebook.

"What are you writing, Carlos?" I asked him.

He looked up and smiled at me. "Private stuff," he said. "It's not about the murders."

Mom closed her notebook and said, "Write down the suspects' names, Jenny, and leave space so we can fill in what we suspect about them."

I did, and Mom said, "Let's talk about Booth first. Thanks to our shrewd detecting, we discovered that he embezzled company stock."

I stopped writing. "Mom," I said, "it wasn't shrewd detecting. You just happened to use an expression that he took the wrong way. You didn't know he was embezzling."

Mom gave a graceful wave of her hand and said, "How I did it doesn't matter. Call it intuition or call it playing a hunch. The truth came out, and that's what we have to work with."

"Do you think Booth killed Porter because he found out Booth had embezzled some of Arnold's company stock?" Carlos asked.

I shook my head. "Booth said that up until now no one knew what he'd done."

"He may have been lying," Carlos said.

"But why would he murder Logan, too?" I asked.

"Logan informed everyone that he was going to write a tell-all book," Mom said.

"But Booth said no one knew about his stock dealings. They wouldn't be in Logan's book."

"It takes us right back to the question, was Booth lying or not?" Carlos said.

Mom rubbed her temples. "This is giving me a headache," she said. "For the moment, let's accept Booth's word as true and go on from there."

"I heard that murderers always lie," Carlos persisted.

"I'm sure they do," Mom acknowledged, "but that isn't helping us complete our list, is it?"

"The next name is Alexa," I broke in.

Mom nodded. "Alexa has too much money in her miscellaneous account. I'd love to see that account if it tells where she bought her clothes. That dress she had on last night was fabulous."

"A logical step now is to check the records for all the money Harmony Chocolates gave to charity, since it's Alexa who wrote the checks," I said. "Do you know if Detective Donovan has asked to see the company's books?"

"I'll ask him tonight. We're having dinner at the Fig Tree, my favorite restaurant," Mom said, smiling. "Jenny, I was wondering . . ."

Carlos chimed in first. "Mrs. Jakes, if you're going out to dinner with Detective Donovan, may I take Jenny out to dinner?"

"Oh," Mom said, looking embarrassed.

"I'd like to go with Carlos," I told her.

"I feel that I need to keep you close by to make sure you're safe," Mom said.

"I'm not a little kid," I answered quickly. "I can take care of myself."

"You can trust me," Carlos said.

"Oh, I know that, dear," Mom told him. "I asked Sam what he knew about you and your family." She stopped herself and looked embarrassed.

I angrily slapped my pen down on the desk. "Donovan already told you he knew Carlos well. And he worked with Carlos's uncle. You didn't have to pry about his family."

"It wasn't prying," Mom said. "I'm a concerned mother."

"It's okay," Carlos said. "I haven't got a record, I don't belong to a gang, and I get good grades. Did Detective Donovan tell you that I'm just a hardworking kid trying to earn a few bucks to pay some bills and help support my grandmother, who's in a nursing home?"

"No, he didn't," Mom said. "But what a fine young man you are."

I studied Carlos. He hadn't exactly said that his grandmother was in a nursing home. He just asked if Donovan had told Mom. So he hadn't actually told something that was untrue—if it was untrue—because maybe it was true. I shook my head. Was I suspicious of Carlos? I had no reason to be.

"If it's all right with you, Mrs. Jakes, I'll take Jenny to a special little restaurant owned by one of my aunts," Carlos said. "Tía Lupita makes the best chiles rellenos in Texas."

"I'm sure they're delicious." Mom beamed at Carlos. "Just bring Jenny back before midnight."

I felt like yelling, *Carlos, ask me if I want to have dinner with you! Mom, stop making plans for me! I can make plans for myself.*

But I didn't. I tried to calm down and changed the subject. "Mom . . . Carlos . . . we're way off track." I realized I sounded grumpy when both Mom and Carlos stopped talking, then turned to look at me in surprise. "I mean," I said in a more reasonable tone, "that we want to finish our list before Donovan gets back."

"Of course," Mom said. "Let's see . . . which suspects have we covered?"

"Booth," I said. "Donovan will probably check the company's financial records, Booth's financial accounts . . . all that. Then we talked about Alexa and wanting to see where the charitable contributions went."

"That leaves Gustave and Claudine," Mom said. "Anyone have some thoughts about either of them?"

"Gustave had a motive for murdering Arnold, who stole his family's candy recipe," I said, "but I can't see any reason for him to murder Porter or Logan."

"Isn't that what detectives do?" Carlos asked. "Go through all the clues and find the murderer?"

"It's not that easy," I said.

"It was for that mystery writer–amateur detective on television. I remember that when viewers were supposed to notice a clue, like, for instance, a jar of jam, the camera zoomed in on it so you couldn't miss it." Carlos grinned.

"Let's start with the money," I said. A thought began forming in my mind, circling around and around and getting bigger and bigger, like a tropical depression out in the Gulf.

"What money?" Mom asked.

"Everybody's money. Money is what this birthday party was all about—Arnold's money and what he was going to do with it. So we need an idea of which of our suspects have money and

156

which don't, and which shouldn't have, and which have more than they should."

"Could you run that by one more time?" Carlos asked.

"It's simple." I was getting excited. "Mom, ask Donovan—"

There was a knock on the door, and Carlos jumped up to open it. "Here he is. You can ask him yourself," Carlos said.

"Ask me what?" Donovan said.

"Mom wants to know if we can take a look at the suspects' financial records, when you get them," I answered. "You did ask to see them, didn't you?"

"I did," Donovan said, "but bank records aren't easily available on weekends. They won't be available until tomorrow."

"We can wait until tomorrow," I told him.

"Considering what has turned up, the records may be irrelevant," he said, and he pulled a plastic bag from his pocket. Inside was a small sheet of notepaper from one of the pads that are found in hotel rooms next to the telephone.

"The crime lab discovered this in Logan's coat pocket," Donovan explained, and read it aloud: " 'I confess to the murder of my father. I have no choice but to take my own life . . . Logan.' "

Mom gasped. I asked quickly, "Did you match the handwriting with Logan's writing on something else?"

"No handwriting. The note was typed," Donovan answered.

"You mean computer printed?" I asked.

Donovan held the envelope closer, peering through the plastic shield. "I don't think so. This looks more like typing than printing. The top of the *e* key is filled in, and there's a repeated smudge on the *r*."

"What about Logan's signature?"

"No signature. Logan's name was typed, too."

"Someone else wrote that note and slipped it into Logan's pocket," I said.

"We can't be sure," Donovan began to explain. "The crime lab will test the paper, try to get fingerprints, hunt for the typewriter on which the note was written, and . . ."

"I can tell you right now the note's a fake," I said.

Donovan looked at me questioningly, so I said, "I mean, *Mom* and I can tell you." I glanced at Mom. "I could see that she recognized what was wrong even before I did." I hurried to add, "We're talking about the wording in the note that says, 'I confess to the murder of my father.' Logan told us he never ever called Porter *father*."

Chapter Sixteen

After praising Mom for her remarkable insight, Donovan left to pass along the fake suicide note to someone in the crime lab. He came back sooner than we had expected and held out the manila envelope. "I made copies of the will," he said. "It will take less time for us to go over it."

"Shouldn't you search the suspects' rooms?" Carlos asked. "If you find the stolen wills, you'll know who took them."

I remembered a lesson I'd learned from Uncle Bill. "The police can't search without warrants," I said, "and there hasn't been enough evidence against any of the suspects to warrant a warrant."

"That's what I was about to say," Mom said. But she thought a moment and added, "Well, maybe not exactly."

"I don't think the person who took the will still has it," I added. "If I wanted it out of the way, I'd destroy it."

"That's what I'm guessing," Donovan said. "As of now we don't know who'd be likely to have stolen the will. We don't even know how, when, where, or why."

"Well, now we can find out," Mom said happily. She and Donovan took the upholstered chairs, while Carlos and I sat on the floor near the sliding glass door. Donovan opened the envelope and withdrew three copies of the will. He took one and passed the other two to Mom and me.

Carlos moved very close to me so he could read over my shoulder. Soon his cheek pressed against mine. I breathed in the warm, spicy smell of his skin and his hair, and it was very hard to concentrate on what I was reading. But Mom sighed and said, "Why do lawyers use so many *whereas's* and *whatfor's*? All they accomplish is to make reading more confusing."

I realized that I couldn't let myself get distracted. Mom needed my help more than I needed to enjoy the closeness of Carlos. I zeroed in on the words, and this time I did my best to pay attention.

Quietly, we read, interrupted only by the little leaps and hops my heart made as I moved too quickly to turn a page and Carlos stopped me by holding my hand still until he had finished reading.

Mom went through the will first. Carlos and I came in a close second, and we all waited patiently until Donovan finished the last page. Something was bothering Mom. I could see it in her eyes, and I expected her to come out with it.

But instead she asked, "How does this will compare with the old will?"

"It's shorter and right to the point," Donovan said. "Let's start with Logan. In the new will his shares of Harmony Chocolates stock weren't given to him outright. They were put into a trust, which he can't—couldn't—touch for fifteen years."

"Poor boy," Mom murmured.

I shivered and tried not to think about Logan's body crumpled on the floor.

"Just as Claudine told us, in the new will she wasn't given any company stock, just a large settlement with yearly payments," Donovan said. "Porter benefited because in the new will he was given complete control of the company."

"Was he killed for revenge?" Mom asked. "It's a perfect motive. The Cooper family in Aspen—"

I interrupted. "The Coopers weren't real, Mom. They were fictional characters in your book *Ski into Danger*." But I was too late. Once again Mom had become Audrey Downing.

"The money didn't matter," Mom said. "She had money, all right. Plenty of it. And so did he. But when he fell in love with the tall blond beauty from Sweden—"

"Mom," I insisted. "Forget what happened in your book. It wasn't true. It was made up. By you. Let's get back to the Harmony family."

Mom looked at me with great patience, which frustrated me even more. "We can learn from many sources," she said graciously. "Besides, I believe we've covered the Harmonys."

"Booth was right. He wasn't mentioned in the will," Carlos said. I knew Carlos was trying to help me out by changing the subject, and I was grateful.

"Booth said he couldn't be," I added, "but what about Alexa and Gustave? Alexa was given a title and full authority over all charitable donations in this will. Was this any different in the first will?"

"No," Donovan said. "As I remember, it was word-for-word the same."

"That leaves Gustave," Mom said. "He was given a pittance, which he could only collect by signing an agreement that he was paid fairly for his family's candy recipe." She turned to Donovan. "What was Gustave's status in the first will?"

"A handsome gift of stock."

"Gustave told us he didn't know what was in the new will," I said, "but now I wonder if he did so much complaining because he really did know. Booth knew everything. Claudine knew what her share would be and maybe Alexa—"

"Don't forget Porter," Mom reminded me. "Porter had seen the will, too." Mom rubbed her chin as she thought. "Logan's stock was tied up so that he couldn't touch it, and Gustave's and Claudine's were taken away," Mom said. "All of them had grievances against Arnold, but I believe that Claudine must be the murderer."

"That might be true if Arnold was the one murdered," I said, "but he wasn't. Why would Claudine murder Porter? And Logan?"

Mom sighed. "On the other hand, maybe we should take Logan's note seriously. If it's true that he killed Porter and then himself, the case would be solved."

At that moment Donovan's cellular phone rang, and he answered it. He grunted a few words, then hung up. "We found the typewriter on which the note was typed," he told us. "It's on the desk of the secretary in the reception room of the hotel's public relations offices. That outer room isn't locked on weekends when no one's there, so anyone could have had access to the typewriter."

"With all the people in this big hotel, weren't there any witnesses who saw the culprit coming or going?" Mom asked.

"None that could be found," Donovan answered. "The public relations offices are deserted on weekends. Also, the person who planted that note on Logan made a big mistake."

"Using the word *father*," I said.

"An even bigger mistake," Donovan told us. "The sheet of paper had no fingerprints on it at all—not even Logan's."

"The culprit wore gloves," Mom said.

"What about the crime lab people who found the note?" Carlos asked.

"They always wear gloves on the scene," Donovan answered.

I noticed that Carlos was scribbling an awful lot in his notebook. While Mom and Donovan continued talking about the fake suicide note, I leaned even closer to see what Carlos had written. "You're writing in Spanish," I complained.

"I'm bilingual," he said.

"I can't read what you've written."

"You're not supposed to. It's private."

I frowned at him suspiciously. "Is this for your newspaper columnist friend?"

"No. This is for me. I'm taking advantage of an extraordinary learning situation."

Carlos's big, beautiful brown eyes were so open and honest and trusting as he smiled at me, that I couldn't help but believe him. I even felt a little guilty for having questioned what he was doing.

In spite of our delicious lunch, I was starving. I was so eager to visit the Riverwalk with Carlos, I grew impatient with Mom and Donovan, who were now arguing about going Dutch.

"But the Fig Tree's expensive," Mom said. "Since we're working together and it could be called a business dinner, I should pay my own share."

"To you, our evening's only a business dinner?"

"Well, not exactly," Mom said. "I just meant that—"

I didn't want to hear their personal problems, so I interrupted. "What have we learned from reading the new will?"

At first Mom, Donovan, and Carlos stared at me. This meeting had to keep going, so I said, "Logan lost control of his company stock. Clau-

164

dine came out of everything financially okay, but she was downsized right out of the company. Gustave was wiped out. The three of them might have had something to complain about, but one of them is dead. Murdered. On the other hand, Porter was given control of the company and Alexa came out the same. What does that tell us about who stole the will?"

"That neither Porter nor Alexa would have had any reason to steal it." Donovan spoke up first.

"But Alexa didn't know what was in the will," Mom said.

"Good point," I told Mom. "I know that you're going to say next that after stealing the will, wouldn't Alexa have been tempted to read it? If she read it and saw how nicely she was treated, she'd have sneaked it back into Booth's briefcase."

"Good thinking, Madeline," Donovan said. He looked at Mom appreciatively. "We've eliminated at least one suspect."

"I don't see how the will figures into the murders," Carlos said. "Arnold wasn't murdered. Porter and Logan were."

"Let's work on that question," I said. "Why did someone want to get rid of Porter and Logan?"

"Logan might have been murdered because he said he was going to write a book and tell all the family and company secrets." Mom started listing the reasons.

"Mom, remember when we first met Porter out

165

in the hall, he wasn't very happy. He had something on his mind," I said. "Didn't he say something about not liking the party?"

Mom nodded. " 'There've been too many parties.' That's what he said."

The rest of the conversation came back to me.
"And then he said, 'Something must be done.' "

"None of the people involved were happy
about the party, except for Arnold Harmony,"
Donovan said.

"We still don't know why Porter Harmony was
murdered," Carlos said.

"Something must be done," I repeated and
tried to catch the thought that kept wiggling
away, out of reach. "Did Porter have something
else to tell?"

Donovan's cellular phone suddenly beeped,
which made all of us jump. He answered, spoke
briefly, then got to his feet. "It's Arnold Harmony," he said to us.

Mom gave a little shriek. "Dead?" she asked.

"No. Sorry I startled you," Donovan answered.
"I was told that Arnold's awake and lucid. He's
agreed to talk to me."

Mom, Carlos, and I jumped up. "Can we go,
too?" I asked.

"I'd like you to be there, Madeline. You've got
insight," Donovan said. He turned to Carlos and
me and added, "You two can come along, but if
Claudine wants you out of the room, then out
you go. Understood?"

I hoped that Donovan would get chunks and

lumps in his mashed potatoes. "Understood," I answered.

When we stepped off the elevator on the fourth floor, heading for suite 487, Mrs. Walker, the same woman from housekeeping, was standing by her cart, angrily telling the hotel's security guard, Mr. Johnson, "Two sheets! Stolen right out of my cart earlier this afternoon! What are people coming to, stealing sheets?"

As she glanced up and saw Mom and me, she grumbled, "Stealing potted plants is bad enough, but at least flowers are pretty. Even thieves like beauty. But stealing unlaundered sheets? Can you tell me why? What is this world coming to?"

Carlos and I looked at each other. "That's where our mantilla person got the white dress," I whispered.

Donovan knocked, and Claudine opened the door to the suite. We walked inside.

Claudine made it obvious that she didn't want us there. I was afraid that she'd tell Carlos and me to leave. However, she totally ignored us—Mom, too—and spoke only to Donovan.

"Arnold understands that Porter was murdered," she said. "He has accepted the fact that it happened, but he wants to know why."

"Claudine, I'll ask my own questions!" Arnold bellowed from the bedroom.

"As you can tell, in spite of his age, there's nothing wrong with his hearing," Claudine said. Her voice dropped to just above a whisper as she added, "We haven't told him about Logan."

"I don't think there's any need to tell him at this time," Donovan whispered back.

"What's all that hush-hushing going on out there?" Arnold called. "If you've got something to say, come in here and say it."

Claudine stepped to one side and motioned Donovan to go ahead. He walked quietly and carefully into the bedroom. Mom, Carlos, and I stuck close to him.

"Don't tiptoe around like I was dead," Arnold shouted.

Mom kissed Arnold on the forehead as she took his hand and said, "Darling, I am so, so sorry about everything that's happened."

Arnold clung tightly to Mom's hand, as though he were afraid to let go. "Madeline," he said, "I know about your reputation for solving murders. I expect you to solve Porter's murder right away."

"Of course," Mom murmured.

Arnold glanced at Donovan. "They told me that he's a homicide detective who's going to help you. Is that right?"

Donovan's eyes turned so dark, any TV meteorologist would have predicted thunderstorms. But Mom winked at Donovan and said to Arnold, "Detective Sam Donovan is allowing *me* to help *him*, Arnold."

"We're working together," Donovan said, his eyes on Mom. "You could say we're a team."

I didn't like the way the conversation was going. I knew I should keep quiet, but I blurted out,

"Cousin Arnold, what did you and Porter talk about last night?"

Arnold's glance landed on me like a laser beam. "Jenny," he said. "Are you trying to take after your mother?"

"I—I just meant—"

He shook his head sadly and sank back into his pillow. "Don't be shy. It's a worthwhile question," he said. "It's why I agreed to talk to Detective Donovan."

"Porter telephoned your suite and arranged to meet with you after the reception," Donovan said.

"But he didn't," Arnold said sadly. "He told me over the phone that he had just learned some damaging information about someone I trusted, and he wanted to talk to me about it before the will was read."

"Did he tell you who this person was?" Mom asked.

"No. He said it was such disturbing news that he'd prefer to tell me in person."

"He didn't give you any idea of what the news was?"

"Not a clue. When it was almost time for Porter to arrive, I sent Adam away so Porter and I would have complete privacy." Arnold's face seemed to shrivel. His voice cracked as he said, "Porter never came."

"Dear one," Mom said as she patted his hand, "we've made great progress in narrowing down the suspects." She straightened and slid into her

Audrey Downing attitude as she added, "I wouldn't be the least bit surprised if Detective Donovan made an arrest very soon."

From where I stood, I could see Claudine give a start, her eyes wide. But it took only a second or two before she had gained control. It happened so fast, I wondered if I had only imagined it.

"Oh, really?" Claudine said. "The others will be glad to hear it."

Mom-Audrey was going strong. She said, "Do you realize that, ideally, a murder should be solved within three days? After three days the trail grows cold, and it's harder to fit the pieces together."

I wished Mom would just be Mom and not get all mixed up with Audrey so that she wouldn't say things she shouldn't. If all the suspects thought that Mom was close to the truth, she might become the next victim!

"There's one important thing you can do to help us," Mom said to Arnold.

"Anything," Arnold said.

"Give Detective Donovan free access to all your computers and files in your office."

"Done," Arnold said. "Adam, give me the phone. I'll make sure you and your detective are allowed into the office right now."

"Now?" Mom asked. "You mean tomorrow morning, don't you?" I knew she was thinking of the elegant dinner she had planned with Donovan.

"No, I mean now," Arnold said. "On Monday

morning the place will be filled with people. There's no time like the present."

Arnold's call took only a minute. "You won't have any trouble," Arnold said to Donovan. "Go ahead."

As Adam moved to turn on a light and close the drapes in the rapidly darkening room, Donovan wrote down the address of Harmony Chocolates.

I took Mom's arm. "Let's go," I said. "We've got some questions that need answers."

"Good girl, Jenny," Arnold said. "I'm counting on you to help your mother."

"Yes, sir," I said, but I had a tight feeling in the pit of my stomach. Desperately I tried to grab the idea I couldn't put my finger on. *We only need the answer to one question,* I thought. *Only one question, and the answer is there. We've seen it. We've talked about it. What is it? When we know it, then we'll know who.*

Chapter Seventeen

As we left the suite, Donovan said, "As for dinner, Madeline, I know a place near the Harmony offices where we can grab a quick ham-
burger."

"Oh, joy," Mom murmured.

I didn't see any need to go with Mom and
Donovan to look at the papers. They could tell
me later what they found. "Carlos and I are going
to his aunt's restaurant now," I said.

Mom looked hesitant, but I could see that she
remembered giving me permission to go. She
gave me a slip of paper with the Harmony Chocolates phone number on it, along with the usual
mother instructions. She kissed my forehead and
said to Carlos, "Please drive carefully."

"I don't have a car," Carlos said. "We're going
to walk. Tía Lupita's place isn't very far from
here."

"Well . . . be careful," Mom said again.

"You be careful, too," I said and glanced pointedly in Donovan's direction as an elevator door opened.

Mom quickly checked to make sure Donovan hadn't seen my look, then shooed us all into the elevator.

The evening was perfect, a light breeze softening the warmth of the day. Carlos took my hand, and as we walked along Broadway with others celebrating Fiesta, we stopped now and then to glance down at the Paseo del Rio. Trees bursting with crops of brilliant colored globes and twinkle lights hung over the walkways. Bright paper flowers mingled with real blooms, and music—combined with laughter—drifted from many open doorways of shops and restaurants.

As we turned back into the stream of pedestrians, I brushed against a woman who was wrapped in a huge, lacy black mantilla. "I'm sorry," I said, but without speaking she turned away from me.

Was she the masked mantilla person from the hotel? I couldn't see her face, but there was no sign of skirts made out of sheets. I put her out of mind, then said to Carlos, "After dinner, let's walk along the river with the tourists."

Carlos grinned. "You're a tourist."

"Not tonight," I said. "Tonight I belong right here. I'm a part of all this."

As Broadway curved away from the river, Carlos let go of my hand. He rested his arm across my shoulders, his head close to mine, and we strolled along the busy street as though we had all the time in the world. Where we were going I

173

didn't know or care. I was aware that we turned down a side street and then another, and stopped in front of a tiny house with one window and a very large front door. A sign hung over the door: TÍA LUPITA'S.

"Is she your real aunt, or is that just the name of the restaurant?" I asked.

"She's real, and she's my mother's aunt," Carlos said. "Come on inside. I'll introduce you. You'll like her."

Carlos was right. Tía Lupita was short and plump, with a smile almost as broad as her face, and she was very proud of Carlos.

When he told her, "Jenny's mother is the mystery writer Madeline Jakes," Tía Lupita beamed.

"Our Carlos is a writer, too," she said. "He's taking journalism in school. He writes for the school paper."

She chattered on while she led us through the tiny room, with its decor of plants and vines trailing out of clay pots. We arrived at the only table that wasn't taken. She was still praising an embarrassed Carlos for his many talents when a waiter called her to the phone.

I unfolded my napkin and placed it on my lap, all the while staring at Carlos. "So you're on the school newspaper," I said. "These notes you've been taking—"

"I have to take notes so I won't forget. I'm learning how to solve a murder," he said.

"If your school newspaper—"

"Jenny," he interrupted, "I wouldn't waste a

story about a local murder on my school newspaper. I mean, they'd never print it. We only write about games and tournaments and school programs and stuff like that."

"You promised you wouldn't give Mom away."

Carlos reached across the table, took the water glass out of my hands, and held them tightly. "I won't. Remember, I told you that you can trust me."

He waited for me to answer, but I was silent.

"Jenny, don't break my heart," he said, his beautiful brown eyes drooping with sorrow. "Believe me. I won't let you down. I promise."

Maybe it was those brown eyes. Maybe it was the magical evening. Maybe it was the warm, spicy fragrance of cheese enchiladas that was making my stomach rumble and driving me crazy. "I trust you, Carlos," I said and smiled.

He smiled back, his expression as calm and unruffled as the water in my glass.

Oh, Traci, if you could see me now!

Tía Lupita placed on the table in front of us a beautifully arranged platter of what looked like thin pancake sandwiches with melted cheese bubbling out around the edges. Carlos and I let go of each other, our hands doing a disappearing act under the table.

"Just a small taste of chicken quesadillas," she said, "while you're waiting for Carlos's favorite rellenos. They'll be ready soon."

She left, and Carlos and I helped ourselves to the quesadilla quarters. Flaky, spicy, creamy,

175

tender . . . I closed my eyes in pleasure, while at the same time I tried to keep strands of the melted cheese from dribbling down my chin.

Someone was watching me. I could feel it. Quickly I dabbed at my face with my napkin and raised my eyes to glance around the room. All the diners were eating peacefully, intent on demolishing their meals. It was then I spotted him.

"Carlos," I said, "how well known is this restaurant?"

"It's considered one of the best kept secrets in San Antonio," he answered, his mouth full. "Tía Lupita has a loyal following. You'll notice that most of the diners don't look like party-going tourists. They're locals. Why'd you ask?"

"Because," I said, "and don't look now— Booth Dockman is sitting at a table in the corner, over near that woman in the large, black mantilla, with her back to us." For just an instant I thought about the woman I'd brushed against on Broadway. *There must be hundreds of women here dressed for Fiesta in those large mantillas*, I told myself.

Carlos immediately turned and looked at Booth.

"Do you think he followed us?" I asked.

"I don't know," Carlos said. "He lives in San Antonio. He may just like to come here."

"He's not looking in this direction."

"Then he probably doesn't even know we're here."

A waiter, bringing our next course, cut off my view of Booth. When I was able to see Booth again, he was demolishing a bowl of soup. *False alarm*, I thought and immediately forgot Booth as I admired my plate of food.

The chiles rellenos were everything Carlos promised they'd be, and the cheese enchiladas were terrific. But somewhere between the guacamole and the charro beans, I leaned back in my chair with a little moan. "I can't eat another bite," I said.

Carlos wiped a spot of red chili sauce off the end of his nose. "Tía Lupita makes wonderful flan," he said.

"Well, maybe one more bite," I told him. But when the molded flan arrived, that first spoonful of cold, slippery, creamy custard slid down so easily, it wasn't long before I'd eaten all of it.

"Carlos," I said, "I've been thinking."

"You aren't supposed to think while you're eating good food. You're supposed to just enjoy it."

"I did enjoy it, but I can't get my mind off some of the things that just don't seem right, like who would steal the new will."

"We didn't come up with any good ideas. Remember?" Carlos said. "The only suspect we eliminated was Alexa, because her part of the will hadn't changed."

That strange, tickling thought came back. Once again I wondered if it had to do with Porter and something he wanted to tell Arnold, but hadn't.

"Jenny, stop frowning," Carlos said. "Your mom and Detective Donovan are going through stacks of papers right now. They may find something that solves the case. In the meantime, relax. Have fun. Okay?"

"Okay," I said. "Let's go down to the river. And thanks for the wonderful dinner."

"Thank Tía Lupita," he said. "Whenever I come here, dinner's on the house."

After the waiter had cleared the plates away and Tía Lupita, hugging Carlos, had made me promise to come back again, we left the restaurant. We passed the table where Booth had been sitting, but he was no longer there, and a busboy was clearing away the dishes.

Once outside, Carlos and I began to retrace our steps toward the Riverwalk and the hotel.

A full moon was high in the sky, and the small street was quiet and empty, except for the two of us. I was in love with the evening, and the mood of Fiesta, and maybe a little bit with Carlos.

I heard footsteps behind us, and I quickly turned. Unfortunately I didn't know that Carlos was about to put his arm around me, and my sudden movement threw him off balance. He staggered into me, and my back met a brick wall.

"Carlos," I said, trying to peer over his shoulder. "Someone's coming."

Carlos looked in both directions, meanwhile slipping his other arm around me. "No, they're not," he said.

"I heard footsteps."

"No, you didn't. Look. The street's empty." He grinned and added, "You heard the beat of my heart."

I giggled, and before I knew it Carlos was kissing me. It was a warm, light, fun kiss, and tasted like the caramelized sugar sauce on the flan. I kissed him back.

With our arms around each other's waists, we walked a few steps and kissed again. I had my mind totally on Carlos, but something suddenly interrupted me. The wispy thought I'd been trying to catch finally pulled itself together. The answer I'd been looking for bounced into my head with a bang.

With a gasp, I opened my eyes and pulled back.

"Carlos," I said. "I've got it."

"You certainly have," he said and reached for me again.

"No, listen," I said. "It's important. I have to tell you right now."

"Okay, I'm listening," he said.

But neither of us spoke. From down the street came hurried footsteps, and I saw a dark shape running toward us.

"Carlos!" I gasped. "It's the murderer!"

Chapter Eighteen

"Run!" Carlos yelled. He grabbed my hand, nearly pulling me off my feet, and we raced down the next side street to Broadway. The crowds weren't as thick as they'd been earlier, but I felt a lot better with people around us.

I glanced behind us as I stopped, panting for breath, and saw that the person in the dark mantilla was keeping up with us . . . if anything, coming even closer.

Crowds or no crowds, I was terrified, and desperate to get back to the hotel. "Why is someone chasing us?" I asked.

"It's not chasing us. It's chasing *you*, because it's figured it out," Carlos said.

"Figured out what?"

"That when it comes to solving crimes, *you're* the brains and not your mother."

A cluster of people who had climbed the stairs from the river barged out onto the sidewalk and into us. A bleached-blond woman, bulging out of a lime green tank top and shorts, yelled, "Harry! Look! It's that cute bellboy from the hotel!" As she wrapped an arm around Carlos's neck and pulled him into their circle, his hand was torn from mine. "Come on, Carlos. Come party with us," she gurgled.

"Carlos!" I shouted, but he was not only surrounded, he was practically smothered against the woman's shoulder.

I couldn't wait for Carlos to escape. I took off as fast as I could, dodging through groups of party goers. I ran until I smashed against the front desk in the hotel's lobby, gulping in long, shuddering breaths.

"Do you need help?" A woman behind the counter looked at me with concern.

I gasped for breath a couple of times, then found my voice. "Yes," I said. "I need a telephone."

"The phone banks are on your right," the woman told me, but I glanced again at the front doors and shook my head. "I'll never make it," I told her. "Please, dial for me. It's an emergency."

"All right," she said. "What's the number?"

I pulled the scrap of paper out of my shirt pocket and handed it to her. She dialed a phone on her side of the desk, pulled it up, and handed it to me. "It's ringing," she said.

I don't know who answered, but some woman said, "Oh, I'm sorry. Your mother and Detective Donovan just left. I was about to lock up."

"Were they going back to the hotel? Did they

tell you?" I kept my eyes on the lobby doors. What had happened to Carlos? Where was the person in the mantilla?

"I didn't ask, and they didn't tell," she answered.

"They didn't happen to say anything about going out to dinner, did they?"

"They didn't need to. That nice detective brought hamburgers and fries for the three of us."

"Thanks," I said, and repeated my thanks to the woman behind the counter as I handed her the phone. "Could you see if Mrs. Jakes is in our room?" I gave her the room number.

She dialed it for me on a house phone, listened, and shook her head. "No one answers," she said. "Do you want to leave a message?"

"No. That is, *yes*," I said. I glanced over my shoulder and thought I saw the person in the mantilla just outside the glass doors. "Say that Jenny will be in suite 487. Bring Donovan and come as fast as you can."

She repeated the message, and I cautiously walked to the elevators, my knees trembling at every step. Where was Carlos? Where was the murderer dressed in the huge mantilla? Would the person enter the hotel by another door? If so, I could expect an encounter in or near our room. Or Elsie and Mabel's room, where the murderer had found me before. My only safe haven would be Arnold's suite.

An elevator door opened, and I stepped in with others who had been waiting. The door closed, and I leaned back against the elevator wall, breathing a sigh of relief. When we arrived at the fourth floor I stepped out eagerly.

Alexa was there to greet me. "Hello, Jenny," she said. "Did you and your friend have a nice evening out?"

"Very nice," I said, trying to keep my voice steady. I attempted to go around her. "Please excuse me . . ."

"Where are you going?"

"To visit Cousin Arnold."

"That's lovely," Alexa said, "but first, why don't you and I find a nice quiet place for a little chat?"

"No, thanks," I said.

Alexa smiled broadly. "Oh, c'mon," she said and took my arm.

The elevator bell dinged, the elevator doors opened, and I heard Mom say, "There you are, Jenny. We returned as the phone was ringing, but didn't make it in time. However, we received your message." Mom smiled at Alexa as she and Donovan joined us. "You must have been exercising, Alexa dear," she said. "You look a little disheveled."

"I'll see you later," Alexa said to me, ignoring Mom, but Donovan stepped forward.

"Stick around," he said. "I came across some office records involving your department, and I'd like to get some answers. You can help me. So can some of the others."

"Booth, too?" I asked.

"Especially Booth," Donovan said.

Alexa looked at Donovan like a tiger ready for

183

a meal, but she walked with him to the door of suite 487 and waited while he knocked.

I pulled Mom aside and quietly asked, "Did you find a list of Alexa's charities?"

"Yes," Mom said. "That's what Donovan wants to talk to Alexa and Booth about."

Claudine opened the door of the suite, and Donovan turned to Mom. "Are you coming, Madeline?" he asked.

"Mom," I said, "there's something I've got to tell you, first. Please listen."

"In just a minute, Sam dear," Mom said sweetly.

"Sam dear?" I muttered. "Mom, he's got the disposition of a grizzly bear."

"Now, Jenny," Mom said, "you know nothing about grizzly bears. If you'd just—"

I quickly interrupted. "Okay, I'm sorry. Listen, Mom. I've got to tell you what I figured out. It began to come together when I remembered what Gustave said about someone influencing Arnold to change his will. After I thought about it awhile, I knew that person had to be Porter."

I told her the rest that I'd figured out, and then I said, "Now, let's get in there with the others."

At that moment Carlos dashed up. He had lipstick smears on his forehead and sawdust on the knees of his jeans. "Jenny, I'm so glad you're all right!" he said and hugged me.

"Where were you? What happened to you?" I asked.

"That big woman and her friends dragged me with them to Durty Nelly's. I thought she'd strangle me. Anyhow, the minute she let go, I crawled under the table and escaped."

He glanced inside suite 487 and asked, "What's up?"

It's a good thing that Arnold's bedroom was large, because it was crammed with people. Booth and Alexa were crowded next to a grumpy Gustave, while Elsie and Mabel stood like guards, one on each side of Arnold's bed. Since Mabel was nearest to Adam, he'd been pushed into a tight corner. The policewoman clung as close as possible to the doorway.

Claudine stationed herself at the foot of Arnold's bed. "Arnold's doctor left only fifteen minutes ago. He said that Arnold's heart was strong, and he should be out of bed by tomorrow," she told us. "But there's no point in giving him added stress, so will everyone please go into the other room?"

We all began to file into the living room, when Arnold bellowed, "No! Don't leave! I don't want you all in there talking behind my back. I want to hear what's going on!"

We turned and crowded back into the bedroom.

"Besides," Arnold said, "I may have something I want to say."

Mom spoke up. "How about a few questions to answer?"

"What are the questions?" Arnold asked.

Mom turned to Donovan. "If you don't mind, Sam, I'd like to ask my cousin a few basic questions."

"That's our Madeline!" Mabel cried out.

"Go for it, girl!" Elsie cheered. "Let's wrap this case up!"

"Ask your questions, Madeline," Donovan said, although the look he gave Elsie and Mabel wasn't a happy one. "You ask. I'll take notes."

"Thank you," Mom said and beamed at him. She took her glasses from her handbag and put them on, then pushed them up on her hair. "Arnold, dear," Mom said, "did you know that Gustave wanted to sell his family's recipe for chocolates to another candy firm?"

"I'm not surprised," Arnold grumbled, while Gustave pulled himself up as high as he could get and stared down his nose at Arnold. "Gustave also threatened to sue me. Well, he'll see how far that threat got him when my will is read in public."

Mom said, "You changed your will to take away the company stock you planned to leave Claudine because she had . . . uh, overspent. Is that right?"

"Overspent? She's been downright greedy," Arnold said.

Claudine muttered something, but Mom continued. "And didn't you change your mind about giving stock to Logan because of his wasteful and . . . um . . . illegal ways?"

"That's right. All that computer bamboozling. The whole idea was not only stupid, Logan couldn't even carry it off."

"Porter told you about it?"

186

Arnold spoke decisively. "If he learned of anything that would affect the company, Porter always told me."

"He was going to tell you something last night, wasn't he?" Mom asked.

"Yes," Arnold said. For an instant his eyes clouded with pain, and I felt sad, thinking of how he really had loved his son and hadn't shown it, and how Porter hadn't shown his love for Logan, and how all three of them lost out because they were unable to share their feelings.

"Do you know what he wanted to talk to you about?" Mom continued.

"No."

"He told you nothing?"

Arnold's chin wobbled. "He wanted to talk to me even before the reception, but I was excited about the party and didn't want to listen." His throat caught as he said, "I should have listened."

"There was . . . um . . . ," Mom said. She stopped, and I knew she was trying to sort through everything I'd told her.

I whispered to her, "There was just one person left who hadn't lost out in the new will."

"There was just one person left who hadn't lost out in the new will," Mom said. "And that person was Alexa. Porter hadn't discovered her double-dealing until just before the party. Alexa murdered Porter to keep him from telling what she was doing. Then she stole the will because she realized that eventually it would occur to us

187

that she was singled out. She was the only one who came out ahead."

I could hear the gasps. They weren't just from Elsie and Mabel.

"Don't be silly," Alexa said. "I didn't murder anyone."

"You murdered two people—Porter and Logan. You murdered Logan because you knew he was aware of some of your escapades and might figure out the others. Not only that, he planned to mention them in the book he intended to write." Mom spoke sternly, yet sadly, just like the fictional mystery writer on television, or Audrey Downing, or both.

Alexa held her head high and tried to stare Mom down. "What escapades? You don't even know what you're talking about."

"Don't be so sure, darling," Mom said. "You admitted spending a great deal on clothing, and—"

Alexa shrugged. "Everybody knows about that. I even told you."

"Yes, you did, and you hoped we'd keep that in mind and not even attempt to look at your list of charities." Mom adjusted her glasses, cleared her throat, and said, "You interrupted me before I had finished, Alexa. Please allow me to continue."

Alexa no longer looked courageous as Mom went on.

"Dear Arnold was very generous with his donations to charitable institutions, but he should have hired someone to check them out."

"Booth investigated all of them," Arnold interrupted. "He's the one who approved the contributions and the checks."

"Booth?" Mom shot a quick questioning look at me.

I quickly said, "Mom suspected from the first that Booth and Alexa were in the scam together. Alexa set up a fake foundation, Booth made it legal, and large financial contributions were poured into it. The money, of course, ended up in Booth's and Alexa's pockets."

Booth started to bluster as Donovan said, "We have Alexa's list of charitable organizations, and it will be easy to get hold of the signed checks and the financial records we'll need to prove fraud."

Alexa looked scornful. "You'll never convict us of fraud. I represent Harmony Chocolates. I'm well liked by all the right people, including Arnold Harmony. Arnold knows I've represented his company well. He doesn't have to bring charges and put up with a lot of terrible publicity that might hurt his company."

Arnold looked distraught. "I don't like what I've heard, but maybe Alexa is right. Maybe it would be better not to press charges against her." He turned toward Booth and scowled. "Booth, on the other hand . . ."

Donovan added, "It seems that Porter had just learned about Alexa's bogus foundation, so I'm guessing that he hadn't had time to further investigate and discover the part that Booth played."

Alexa interrupted as she faced Donovan.

"Those murder charges Madeline threatened me with are equally foolish. I had nothing to do with either Porter's or Logan's deaths."

Booth suddenly spoke up. "Oh, yes she did. You can see how she just got herself out of the fraud charges, leaving me to take the blame. She's not going to do the same with the murders, though. I won't let her. She committed them, not me. That fruit knife—she was furious, and the knife was handy."

"Don't be absurd," Alexa snarled. "Be quiet!"

But Booth was frightened, and he continued, "Alexa arranged that lunch in suite 485, and she told me how she'd obtained the fortune cookie and the cyanide."

"I told you to shut up, and they'd never be able to prove a thing!" Alexa screamed.

Booth hesitated.

"Oh, yes, they will," I said, jumping in. "Mom intends to ask Detective Donovan to have the calls to your room traced. Records will show that Porter called your room from his to tell you that he had made an appointment to tell Arnold about your scam. He didn't call Booth. He called *you*, Alexa."

Alexa didn't answer, but Booth fell apart. "Alexa told me what Porter had said," Booth told us. "I was afraid the . . . uh . . . donations were over, but she said, 'Don't worry. Porter won't tell Arnold. I'll stop him from telling tales ever again.' "

I hoped no one would challenge what I'd said

about tracing the calls. I knew, from what Uncle Bill had once told me, that hotels never keep records of guests' calls within the hotel. They only keep track of the outside calls guests are charged for. I looked at Mom and then at Donovan, but neither of them reacted to what I had said. They were intent on Booth's eyewitness confession.

Donovan stepped to Alexa's side, drew her arms behind her, and slapped handcuffs on her wrists. "We'll take you downtown for further questioning," he said. "I'm sure you both have more to tell us." He motioned to the policewoman to handcuff Booth.

"Nice work," the policewoman murmured to Mom as she passed her.

"We make a good team, Madeline," Donovan said. For a minute I thought he was going to kiss her as he paused on his way out the door.

"Yes, we do," Mom answered warmly and put her glasses back into her purse.

Elsie and Mabel rushed up and hugged Mom. "You're just like the mystery writer on TV!" Elsie cried.

"We're so proud of you, Madeline," Mabel said.

"I knew you could do it, Madeline!" Arnold called out. "Thank you!"

Mom hugged me as we left. "I did it! I really truly solved a murder!" she said. "Aren't you proud of me?"

"You bet I am, Mom," I answered, but I

thought about all that had happened to *me*, not to her.

"I'm proud of you, too, Jenny," Mom said. "You were a big help to me."

Mom-Audrey really thinks she solved the murders, I thought.

I realized when we opened the door to the hall that Claudine had kept pace with us. Claudine glanced back, making sure we were out of Arnold's hearing, then said, "I suppose you think I should thank you, too, but I won't."

Mom looked surprised, and Claudine said, "All the personal problems between Arnold and me— they're going to be made public, aren't they?"

"Not by me," Mom said.

"You're not going to write some big tell-all kind of story?"

"Of course not," Mom said. "That's not what I write. I write mystery novels."

Claudine visibly relaxed and gently touched Mom's arm. "Then thank you," she said quietly.

Mom hesitated, then asked, "Claudine, do you remember a delightful musical teapot that Agnes used to use? A dear little teapot decorated with pink roses and tiny violets?"

Claudine thought a moment, then laughed. "That silly old thing? I remember it. Agnes must have had dreadful taste. When I married Arnold, I cleaned out a whole cupboard of ugly things and gave them all to the Goodwill. Why do you ask?"

At first Mom looked hurt. *Poor Mom,* I

thought. *She really wanted that teapot.* Now I understood her bewildered expression after she had read the new will and found that Arnold hadn't even mentioned the teapot.

But Mom was resilient and I could see her mind slowly shift gears. "Hmmm . . . a missing teapot," she said. "Who knows where it is and what it holds? It may just show up someday in one of my stories." She pulled out her notebook and made a note.

I looked around for Carlos, but he was nowhere in sight. At first, I was puzzled. Then I began to realize what Carlos must be doing. The more I thought about it, the angrier I grew.

"I'll meet you at the room, Mom," I said. "There's something important I have to take care of."

I found Carlos just where I thought he'd be—at the phone bank next to the lobby.

"Yeah," I heard him say. "I have the inside story. I was with it every step of the way. Let me write it. It'll be an exclusive for the *Light*."

I couldn't believe what I was hearing. My stomach clutched, my head hurt. I began to ache all over. Carlos, a sneak!

"Of course I expect to be paid," Carlos said into the phone. "We can talk about how much when I come in tonight to write the story."

That was the last straw. I punched him in the back and said, "I hate you!"

193

Startled, Carlos turned and faced me. "Gotta go," he said to whoever he was talking to at the newspaper. "I'll be there in fifteen minutes."

"If I had a choice, you'd be at the bottom of the river in fifteen minutes," I told him.

"Jenny, listen," Carlos pleaded.

"I did listen to you," I said. "You promised to protect Mom's reputation, and I believed you."

"Jenny—"

"I trusted you."

"Please, Jenny. You don't understand."

"Yes, I do," I told him. "You want to be a journalist, and this is your big chance."

"It is, but—"

"Are you really going to write about what happened here?"

"Yes," he said, "But—"

The hurt and disillusionment I felt were too much to handle. I turned and ran for the elevators.

Chapter Nineteen

I tried three times to call Traci. I became more and more miserable as each time no one answered. Mom's life was about to be ruined, my life had just gone down the drain, and I needed a good friend to talk to. Finally, I took a hot shower and went to bed. It was late, and I was exhausted.

It didn't help any that Mom was so pleased with herself that she couldn't stop reliving every step of her success. It broke my heart that when next morning's newspaper came out, her reputation as a successful mystery-writer sleuth was going to be shattered.

Maybe if I got up first and hid the newspaper . . . No. Everybody in San Antonio would read it anyway. If Carlos's story was any good, it could even be picked up by the wire services, and everybody in the United States—the world even— would read the worst about Mom.

I was sure I'd never get to sleep, but I dreamed about bells ringing and Mom laughing.

It seemed like only a few minutes before a brilliant daylight woke me. I squinted through half-closed eyes to see that Mom had opened the drapes wide.

"Hop out of bed, sweetie," Mom said. "Room service will bring our breakfast in just a couple of minutes."

As I sat up and swung my feet over the edge of the bed, Mom said, "Elsie just telephoned. She told me that there's a wonderful story in this morning's newspaper about how Porter's and Logan's murders were solved."

I groaned. "Mom, let me explain. Carlos—"

"Yes, I know. Carlos wrote the story," Mom said. "Isn't that wonderful? That dear, modest, talented boy!"

Wonderful? Modest? Talented?

A brisk knock came at the door, and I dove under the covers. But the minute the table had been set up and Mom had signed the bill, I scrambled out. "Did he bring a newspaper?" I asked.

"Yes. Here it is," Mom said.

It was a front-page story, complete with Carlos's byline and a photo of Mom's smiling, glamorous face.

We read the story together—a story about a mystery writer who was also a talented detective. Mom came out looking great. I showed up in the story only as her loyal sidekick.

"Oh, Mom," I said when I'd finished reading. "This story is exactly what I hoped it would be. It makes me so happy." Then, remembering the terrible, awful, horrible things I'd said to Carlos, I wanted to cry.

I snatched up the phone and punched the two numbers that would connect me to the bellmen's desk. A voice answered, "How can I help you, Mrs. Jakes?"

"When does Carlos Martinez come on duty?" I asked.

"He's on duty right now. Do you need him?"

"I will later," I said. "Thanks."

I think I must have showered and dressed in record time. If getting ready in the morning had been an Olympic event, I would have won the gold.

Mom was still in her robe sipping coffee when I kissed in the direction of her forehead. "Bye, Mom. I'll be right back," I said.

She blinked at me in surprise. "Where are you going?"

"Just down to the lobby. I'll be back soon."

"Jenny, my sweet," Mom said, "you don't have to return to school until next Monday. Would you mind if we spent a few leisurely days here in San Antonio? Once Donovan finishes the paperwork, he'll have a couple of days off. He'd like to show us around the city."

Sam Donovan, I thought, realizing that sooner or later his name would come up. There were some good things about Donovan, but on the whole . . . it was obvious that Mom needed some guidance where he was concerned. You couldn't be abrupt with mothers in their forties, so I'd have to pick the right place and the right time for our little talk.

"Decide when you want to leave, and I'll call the airlines when I get back," I said. I shut the door behind me.

Waiting at the elevators, which were incredibly slow, I jabbed the *down* button impatiently. Finally, an elevator arrived and I hopped on.

As the door opened at the lobby, I spotted Carlos pushing an empty luggage cart in my direction. I ran up to him.

Carlos just glanced at me and kept going. He pushed the *up* button for an elevator.

"Carlos, I'm sorry for all the terrible things I said to you last night."

"I tried to explain what I was going to write," he said. "You wouldn't let me."

An elevator door opened, and Carlos pushed the cart inside. He didn't attempt to make room for me, so I climbed in through the end of the cart and crouched down, hanging on to the brass poles.

"I was upset," I told him as the elevator began to move. "And I was scared."

"You didn't trust me."

"At first I didn't," I admitted, "and that made everything worse. I knew I cared an awful lot about you when my head hurt and I felt sick to my stomach and began to ache all over."

Carlos pushed the elevator *stop* button and stared at me in surprise. "A headache and sick to your stomach? And aching all over? That's how you feel when you care about someone?"

"That's how I feel when I care about someone, and I've done something so incredibly stupid that he might never want to see me again."

"This caring about someone," Carlos asked. "Is it like falling for someone really hard?"

"Kind of," I answered.

Carlos leaned into the cart, wrapped his arms around me, and kissed me.

When Carlos let go of the *stop* button, the elevator began to move, but neither of us noticed. It suddenly came to a stop on its own, and the door opened.

Before us stood another bellman with a cart piled with luggage. He held the door open, grinned, and said, "Well, well, if it isn't Carlos Martinez, hardworking bellman."

"You're only half right," I said. "He's better known as Carlos Martinez, journalist."

We pushed the cart into the hall just in time to see Elsie and Mabel trotting after their luggage cart and bellman, who waited for them at the elevators. They praised Carlos for his story and hugged us both.

"Let us know the next time," Elsie said to me.

"The next time?"

"You know," Mabel said. "The next time Madeline's on hand when someone's murdered. You know, like that TV mystery writer always is."

"Okay," Carlos answered, "but remember, the victim's usually a relative."

199

Shocked, they scurried down the hall. "Car-los," I said, "we're staying here a few more days, so if you have any time off . . ."

Carlos's smile lit up his face. It didn't take any detecting skills to know that the rest of the week was going to be great.

About the Author

Joan Lowery Nixon has been called the grande dame of young adult mysteries and is the author of more than a hundred books for young readers, including *Don't Scream*; *Spirit Seeker*; *Shadowmaker*; *Secret, Silent Screams*; *A Candidate for Murder*; *Whispers from the Dead*; and the middle-grade novel *Search for the Shadowman*. She is the 1997 president of the Mystery Writers of America and is the only four-time winner of the Edgar Allan Poe Best Young Adult Mystery Award. She received the award for *The Kidnapping of Christina Lattimore*, *The Séance*, *The Name of the Game Was Murder*, and *The Other Side of Dark*, which also won the California Young Reader Medal. Her historical fiction includes the award-winning series The Orphan Train Adventures.

Joan Lowery Nixon lives in Houston with her husband.